Nightcrawlers, Bait and Beer To Go

About the Author

Although he can recall at least twenty different types of jobs he has had through the years, most of Hal Shymkus' business career has been involved in communications. After being an editor of the Chicago Heights *Star*, he spent thirty years with Cummins Engine Company in the management of advertising, graphics, and promotion, among other responsibilities.

He was born in Chicago and has first-hand knowledge of the Depression and World War II, where he was stationed in Foggia, Italy.

In 1983 he retired early, not entirely to pursue his enthusiasm for fishing and golfing, but to do advertising consulting and freelance writing. His material has appeared in *Sports Afield, Field & Stream, MidWest Outdoors, Game & Fish, Great Lakes Fisherman, Senior Golfer, Western People*, and other publications.

He and his wife, Mary Beth, live in Columbus, Indiana.

Nightcrawlers, Bait, And Beer To Go

A Collection of Stories that Tickle the Tummy

By
Hal Shymkus

Library of Congress Catalog Card Number: 90-50960

ISBN: 0-923568-19-0

Illustrations by Larry J. Monroe

Typesetting by
LaserText Typesetting
3886 Sheldrake Avenue ⌂ Okemos, Michigan 48864

PUBLISHED BY

Wilderness Adventure Books
320 Garden Lane
Box 968
Fowlerville, Michigan 48836

Manufactured in the United States of America

For Karl and Walt, fishing friends for a quarter of a century . . .

For my wife, who never said I couldn't go . . .

And for the many fishermen who unknowingly made this book a reality.

The illustrations in this book are the work of Larry J. Monroe. This native Hoosier was born in southern Indiana in the year of the great flood. He spent his early years on a farm where he gained an appreciation for hunting and fishing. Except for an art correspondence course, most of Larry's graphics ability has been self-taught. He and his wife, Doris, are the parents of five boys and a girl.

"Here is the basket; I bring it home to you. There are no great fish in it. But perhaps there may be one or two little ones which will be to your taste. And there are a few shining pebbles from the bed of the brook, and ferns from the cool, green woods, and wild flowers from the places that you remember. I would fain console you, if I could, for the hardship of having married an angler: a man who relapses into his mania with the return of every spring, and never sees a little river without wishing to fish in it. But after all, we have had good times together as we have followed the stream of life towards the sea. And we have passed through the dark days without losing heart, because we were comrades."

From *FISHERMAN'S LUCK* by Henry Van Dyke

Contents

Introduction

It has always disturbed me to pick up a book, read the superlative words on the jacket or the introduction, then after reading a few of the chapters discover that the contents only vaguely coincide with what you thought the book was going to be.

So, before you venture too much further in this book, I want to tell you what *Nightcrawlers, Bait, and Beer To Go* is all about.

It is not a book about how to fish, where to fish, when to fish, and what to use. There are many excellent references on the art of angling that can be found in most libraries, bookstores, and sporting equipment supply outlets that will provide this kind of information. There are even video cassettes available that dramatize clearly the rudiments of fishing. So, if you are just getting started and want to learn more about the sport of fishing or want a refresher on how to improve your skills, turn to these sources.

In hopes you haven't shut the cover of this book and gone off to your local library, bookstore or sporting equipment supply outlet, let me tell you what you will find in this book.

This is a collection of stories, anecdotes, experiences and memories people have had through fishing. It is about all those humorous and serious circumstances long remembered after the catch. This book talks about Knobby's Place. Although this is a fictitious name for a specific location where hundreds of people have gone for years to get away from "things," to commune with nature, to share a common activity with their fellow man, and to find time to fish, Knobby's

Place actually is wherever you go fishing for whatever period of time and with whomever.

The characters at Knobby's Place are a composite of many with whom I have had the pleasure of fishing. They are very real in every respect. Perhaps you will recall one or two of them from your own fishing experiences.

You should keep in mind all of the stories at Knobby's Place are based on actual incidents that have taken place while fishing. Sure, some of them have been dramatized somewhat and even slightly embellished to some degree, but what fisherman has not been known to stretch the truth a tad or two. It's been said that fishermen, in general, are kind of strange people who do strange things and end up having strange experiences. You'll find this true when reading *Nightcrawlers, Bait, and Beer To Go.*

Some people advocate fishing is competition matching man against fish in their environment; the thrill of catching a trophy size fish on the lightest of tackle; the rewarding experience of returning a good size keeper back to its waters. There is no question about these thrills and satisfaction. They are very personal and self-fulfilling. There is no question about the competition. Those Big Fish contests offering more and more money are attracting more and more fishermen.

Look at the popularity of fishing, the revenue it brings in, and the employment it generates. A nationwide survey indicates that over 22 million men and 9 million women rank freshwater fishing as one of the top ten most popular activities. And fishing can only increase in popularity.

In most instances, however, if people were asked why they fish, the response would be because they so much enjoy what fishing does to them and for them. It brings people together, closer. It is a kind of therapy you get from wetting a line. It is the preparation, the anticipation, expectation, the feeling that tomorrow will be even better. It's like the adage that says, "Give a man a fish and he eats for a day, but teach him to fish and he'll eat for a lifetime."

How often have you seen youngsters fishing from the banks of a farm pond beaming with a virgin excitement of hooking a prize catch? And if they don't, they will have had the undeniable experience of sharing their young concerns and feelings about growing up, about life, and about the fun of just being there. It's summed up in a passage from the book *At Broad Ripple* that goes like this, "I bait my hook and cast my line, and feel the best of life is mine."

Ever go fishing with your father when you were young or not so young? And father, if you haven't taken your son or daughter fishing, do so because you will never forget or regret those times. You will find your offspring will have a lot to say about things. There is a bumper sticker that reads, "Have You Hugged Your Kid Today?" How about a bumper sticker that reads, "Have You Taken Your Kid Fishing Lately?"

I can remember my father so patiently telling me not to throw stones in the water while "we" were fishing. I believe it was some place along the banks of the Kankakee River, and he said it in the softest, most quiet and sensitive voice I ever heard him use. And I can recall to this day the saying he often used when I didn't catch anything. "You gotta spit on the worm and hold your mouth right."

I wondered then what spitting on a worm and holding one's mouth had to do with fishing and I am still perplexed, but it was one of his favorite expressions so I continue to use it with people I fish with.

My wife told me it was about time I explained the facts of life to our young son and I should do this on a picnic to a lake we had planned. Well, there we were on this small lake and I finally organized my thoughts on what I was going to say about the birds and bees. Right at that moment my son was intently watching his bobber start to quiver. I guess he was holding his mouth right as I told him to do. Gathering courage I blared out, "David, what do you know about babies, like where they come from?" To which he replied without ever taking his eyes from that nervous cork bobber, "Dad, I know all about those things from school. Now, I think I've got a bite."

Sure enough he did and was he ever pleased and proud pulling in a bluegill. As for me, I was pleased and proud we had our little discussion about the reproductive system.

Let me tell another story how fishing brings people closer together and breaks down barriers. In the group of guys I fish with it is customary to say a blessing before the evening meal. Whenever possible one of us will use the traditional Lutheran, Presbyterian, or Methodist words depending on whose turn it is. We have done this in lodge dining rooms, in our own small cabin, at a camp outpost, and in the open under the evergreens. One year we had the experience of fishing with two elder Ojibway Indians on one of their wilderness lakes in Northern Ontario. It was as remote an environment as we had ever experienced before and the first day there we were apprehensive about a lot of things. We all gathered for the evening meal in a cabin that served as the kitchen. It was a delicious meal prepared by the oldest of the two Ojibways who indicated it was time to eat by simply saying, "Ready." We sat down at a picnic table arrangement and said we would like to say a blessing. We bowed our heads and folded our hands to help them understand. They followed. The blessing was given and we really didn't expect the Ojibways to understand what was fully being said but when the word, "Amen" was used they both said it as we did. The third night out we asked them if they would like to say the blessing. The oldest smiled and we learned later that this sincerely pleased them to be invited to give the blessing. We all bowed and the oldest said the blessing in Ojibway and in what sounded to be more profound words than ours. We now only knew the last word and said "Amen" along with them.

This was an experience brought about through fishing which emotionally linked all of us closer to one another.

A friend of mine was anti-fishing, anti-hunting for as long as I knew him. It was his contention that man with his modern devices could outwit animal, fish, fowl. He sometimes went to extremes pontificating the virtues of abolishing hunting and fishing. He did this quite often just to get my dander up, but more than occasionally we would get into long, drawn-out discussions during whiskey sipping evenings about this type of pasttime. The point I always tried to make was that it wasn't necessarily the thrill of hooking a fish or downing the bird, it was all the programming beforehand that stimulated the excitement. More importantly, it was the companionship with others on the trip that made it seem worthwhile. And lastly, I was not that skilled anyway where I would have an advantage.

This repartee would go on and on until one year after he and his wife had returned from a vacation. Oddly enough, the couple they had gone with talked him into going fishing for half a day on a charter boat. I will never forget the conversation we had when we met again.

"You won't believe it but I finally went fishing."

"You gotta be kidding! Do any good?" I knew I should not have phrased it exactly that way but it was a typical fisherman's response.

"If you mean did I catch any fish, the answer is no, not even a bite," he commented.

"Well, now what do you think?" I asked.

He said, "You know, the four of us talked about things I never thought we would. About our kids, our jobs, ourselves, our aspirations, concerns, our future. I guess the only thing we didn't cover was our sex life, and I thought we were coming close to that also."

Don't overlook fishing with your wife either. It can open up doors that are often closed without either one of you actually knowing it. Ed Howe has been quoted about the husband-wife relationship, "A woman who has never seen her husband fishing doesn't know what a patient man she has married."

My anti-fishing friend has since retired and has fished from Florida to Canada. He has started a library on various aspects of fishing, has some of the finest tackle available, recommends the type of equipment to use for whatever species of fish, knows all about weather conditions—even about the dark of the moon. He has also started a collection of antique fishing lures. In other words, he has a full-blown case of the "Fishing Pox" disease that is contagious to anyone his age or younger.

So, what's this book all about?

Maybe you have heard the expression, "Fish or cut bait." I am not certain of the exact source of this reference and have heard many opinions. Several have told me that it more commonly means, "Just don't stand (sit) there, do something!" If you are not going to fish, be productive by cutting bait for those who do. With that in mind I wanted this book to cover what happens to people while they are fishing, how they react to certain situations, the things they do which they would not normally do. A loosening up. Being yourself. Getting an identity.

Ever wonder why some fishermen look the way they do? Grubby kinds of wearing apparel. Goofy hats, camouflage outfits like they intend to ambush the fish. Growth of facial hair. Sheath knife tucked to their belt. Some call this "macho". Call it anything you want but it gives them something to identify with and a commonality with others of that ilk which is hard to come by in a business-as-usual environment. It's the same with the Abercrombie & Fitch guy. A tackle box as big as a house trailer. Bass boots, L. L. Bean undershorts. Fenwick, Browning, Orvis rods. A deluxe Dobbs hat laden down with lures of all kinds. No wonder so many fishermen come home with headaches. But these are the important things that bring a lot of close people closer.

On one trip far back in the boonies our group and another were the only ones fishing a remote lake. We each occupied a rough tent-type cabin. It was fairly wild country and the facilities were primitive at best. We never saw much of the other group of fishermen even though our cabins were not very far from each other. We would hear them laughing and talking sometimes far into the night. All they wanted to do was play bridge, eat, and drink. Fishing was undermost in their minds even though this was one of the most productive waters in the entire area. Keep in mind that this place was very remote, accessible only by float plane with the only communication being a towel hung out on a pole by the dock which was supposed to indicate to a passing plane that you wanted something, that is, if a plane passed, the weather was favorable to spotting the towel, and if you still wanted what you were needing. After a long day on the water our group usually plunked down to a scotch or bourbon to ease the aches and pains of sitting all day in the boat. One night following our evening meal and ample toddies we decided to wander over to the other cabin to strike up some friendly talk about the fishing. Would you believe they were having smoked oysters with their champagne. They had reduced their fishing gear and clothes to the barest minimum in order to make room for these types of delicacies. This gave them something only they could experience together along with a few of us others.

There are a lot of stories like these. The chapters in this book highlight many of them at Knobby's Place and it is like what I've been trying to tell you in this introduction. It is the people who make fishing the experience it is. Whether it be river, lake, creek, stream, brook, pond, pothole, canal, inlet, bay or whatever water, there is a togetherness that is found only by being there.

Fishing is ageless. Christ's four disciples understood. It is worldly like the last line from a Chinese proverb: "If you wish to be happy forever, learn to fish."

My favorite is summed up in the American Indian saying, "God does not charge time spent fishing against a man's allotted time span."

I once crawled up a bank on the Kentucky River on a mission to get gas for an empty tank. Our boat was pulled up to what looked to be a trail that angled through the underbrush and up a steep rise. It was a hot August day full of pests and pollen. By the time I got to the top of the rise, I was truly pooped. The trail I took led to a country dirt road where I sat down and caught my breath. Recovering I finally headed east on the country road not wanting to look into the sun. After what I judged to be three miles at least, I came upon a general, all-purpose type store. The sign in the window comforted me as soon as I saw it. "Nightcrawlers, Bait, and Beer To Go." I had seen no one until I went inside the store. The people running the place were a little surprised seeing a dusty, tired individual bedecked in a T-shirt, shorts and sneakers carrying an empty gas tank, but only momentarily. They became as friendly as the litter of pups playing on the floor. I told them of my dilemma. They gave me some gas that they had to siphon from one of their vehicles in the back. They also gave me a cold beer. And I bought a six-pack for the guys waiting in the boat. These kind people whom I had never seen before and probably never will again cranked up one of their pick-up trucks and carted me back to the trail that led to the river. The hospitality and friendliness was incomparable. I shook hands, said an appreciative "thanks," and started to edge myself down the steep trail. When I got to our boat I was pleased to be able to hand over the filled gas tank and the six pack of beer. You know what the first comment was, "What took you so long?"

Funny, but I expected that reaction.

I hope you enjoy these stories.

1 | Knobby's Place

Lake of Six Rivers is the official name appearing on state and county maps and listed in other documents. It received this designation sometime between 1930 and 1940 after a huge dam was constructed at the end of a series of long and heavily wooded valleys. The purpose of the dam was to control the rampaging water from six rivers that spilled over their banks, especially in the spring and fall, and flooded vast areas to the south. You could see evidence of these floodings in the eroding countryside, diminishing farmland, and flourishing swamps with dying and decaying timber left standing naked.

The outcome of all this dam development was a vast water system in a beautiful wilderness setting with over 120 miles of shoreline not counting various backwaters. It took about four years for Lake of Six Rivers to fill substantially, and while this process was taking place it was noticeable where islands, fallen timber, brush, rock formations, weed beds, and sandy beaches would ultimately provide an ideal fishing environment. You could also imagine how readily the fish would propagate in all this water.

When the body of water reached the prescribed level the dam then controlled the rise and fall of that level. During extra dry weather the water level was lowered in order to provide a reasonable amount of water for farm irrigation miles and miles away. Then, when heavy rains inundated the area the dam managed how high the water would get by the amount let over its spillway. At times some people felt this commercial adjusting of the water level affected the fishing. That theory was always difficult to prove but it did add a different personality to the shoreline whenever the rising and falling process occurred.

Once people started coming frequently to fish Lake of Six Rivers word spread quickly about the preponderance of fish. It was like an angler's paradise. More and more people from outside the county and state started coming here regularly, but you have to remember that back in those days not every other vehicle had a trailer hitch to pull a boat. Actually only a few of the natives had boats and they were extremely selective about who would use them. That meant many fishermen did bank fishing because of the scarcity of boats. This is when Knobby started in business—but that is getting somewhat ahead of the tales about Knobby's Place.

Once the lake filled up only two of the six rivers retained something from their original identity, and only these two rivers continued to be fished as a river instead of as winding depths in the lake system. The other rivers were completely submerged. All six rivers contributed not only to create the Lake of Six Rivers but each of them also had a hand in molding the history of this area, some of them in an unusual and tragic way. A word or two about these rivers is appropriate.

The Flatrock River was named for exactly what its bottom contained—nothing but a bunch of flat, water worn, slippery rocks. It was shallow and fast and apparently not good for much except for seining minnows, but its water was cool and choice for drinking on a hot summer day. Its shallowness allowed Indians and settlers easy fording in this part of the valley, and a long time ago Flatrock was considered good for trout fishing especially where it merged with the Driftwood River along the scattered large boulders and swirling pools. Even today some people try fishing for trout in these waters but they primarily use it as a warm up to more productive streams.

Natives think of the Flatrock more in terms of the satchel of money that was found in the roots of a cottonwood tree that angled out from a bend in the river. The Tymstra boys uncoverd the bag one day as they were skipping stones in the water trying to see who could skip one completely across to the opposite bank. One of the boys reached for a stone and found the bag. As boys, and others would naturally do, they opened the bag and saw all the bills. There were several thousands of dollars all neatly wrapped in that satchel. They ran home as fast as one of their skipping stones, and told their father and mother and showed them the money, and that's when trouble started. Old Dorval Tymstra insisted on keeping the money but his wife insisted on going to the sheriff. Dorval won out for the moment until they could resolve their differences. The boys now wondered why they didn't keep the money and not say anything. Dorval hid the money satchel in their barn. A few nights later a violent storm blew in, lightning struck the barn and set it afire. There was nothing left but ashes.

You could also readily understand why the Driftwood River was called what it was. In the spring the rising, rushing waters tore out foliage faster than a modern day bulldozer. Trees piled up one on another causing the river to dam up pockets of ponds. Then another flood would force more trees and brush on the pile and eventually the course of the river

was rerouted but it created wide backwater areas. The land bordering the Driftwood was ideal for wildlife and became a mecca for hunters and trappers. Practical use of the river for transportation was dangerous since navigation around swirling eddies and unsuspecting currents could suck a boat into sunken logs. Although no fatalities seem to have been recorded, there were many stories about drenchings and destroyed boats.

One strange incident with the Driftwood occurred during a typical spring flood when its force continued to eat away at a bank in a turn of its course. Once the flooding subsided somebody found what appeared to be an Indian burial site. The skeletal remains uncovered by the erosion. Simply little more than that was ever recorded in the annals.

Stillman's River was the biggest contributor to the entire flowage because it was the largest and deepest of all six rivers. It was winding with a slow current along stretches of tree lined banks. Oldtimers always remarked about this river having the best largemouth and smallmouth bass, walleye, and northern pike fishing in the country. It is one of the rivers that still fingers its way into the water system and contains the best spawning waters.

It played an important part in the early history of this area by saving the lives of the Stillman family. A holocaust of a fire hit the area suddenly one autumn destroying everything in its path. The strong wind and tinder-like conditions fueled a fiery onslaught that overpowered forests, farms, and wildlife. It was certain the Stillman family of seven would perish as the blaze swept toward their farm. They ran as fast as they could to the large river and jumped in. They found they had company. Many of their farm animals had already reached these saving waters. From that time on it was always known as Stillman's River.

The Duval River flowed into Stillman's River and was named after the French influence around these parts and one family in particular. As the story goes, one of the Duval daughters was seduced by a hot-blooded, red haired Irish lad by the name of Bill Shaughnessey. The two of them secretly were thick as thieves contrary to their families' wishes and knowledge. Although the young couple believed they were destined to be together forever, the Duval girl had planned on losing her virginity in a more gossamery setting than under a hickory tree.

When the Duval men found out they tracked down young Shaughnessey, whipped his butt, shaved his head of all its handsome, thick, bushy red hair, and sent him running out of the county. A few days later, however, his body was found floating in this river. The Duvals claimed complete innocence affirming that they last saw Shaughnessey high-tailing it up the hills. The Shaughnessey clan wasn't buying this story and wanted their pound of flesh. What was about to become a first-class, full-scale feud was abated when Jack Tackett, a laconic recluse known as Jack the Bum, came wandering into town to replenish his stock of 100 proof cough medicine and heard about the impending shoot out. Jack had enough sense and sobriety at the time to tell the sheriff that young Red (as Shaughnessey was most often called) had stopped off at his cabin a few days before and joined him for supper. That's how Jack found out about the whipping and saw the results of the haircut. Red left the following day and Jack surmised that he must have slipped on one of the ridges, fell into the river, and drowned. That's how the sheriff also surmised it and the feud never openly got off the ground. But continuing hard words and minor altercations spark up occasionally among these two families even today.

The Duval girl was sent away to serve penitence and lived with her notorious aunt many miles away and it was a long time before she ever showed up around here again but when she did, "Oo-la-la."

The Duval River had more romance and intrigue than the other rivers besides having some excellent fishing holes but you have to work to find them since they are now all covered by the water system.

Little Porcupine River was not much to talk about from a fishing standpoint. It was one of those rivers used mostly by the younger set for skinny dipping and spooning along the banks on a moonlit night. Much of the conversation about this river started out with, "Remember when we used to jump bare ass into Hogan's pool on the Little Porc?" or "Your father proposed to me when we were parked along the Little Porc."

Today you hear mostly, "Follow the Little Porc to Pine Island and fish the river around there." Problem is that unless you know the original river course it is difficult to find the Little Porc in this vast flowage. Its backwaters spread out from the water system and is excellent for drift fishing.

The last of the six rivers that formed the Lake of Six Rivers was called Sagamay. It also flowed into Stillman's. The Ojibway Indians gave it this name because it was a breeding ground for mosquitos and Sagamay means "mosquito" in Ojibway language. Before becoming part of the total confluence, the Sagamay wound its way through marshy ground and thickly populated cottonwood trees. The Indians used the river primarily for gathering wild rice and for transportation to Stillman's where they did their fishing.

Viewing the whole layout now it is impossible to imagine how the six rivers worked their way in and around the hills and valleys and forests. One wonders if God had been the architect of the original plan. He purposely hid the dark blackish-blue body of water in a wilderness setting camouflaged and surrounded by evergreens and hardwoods. He stocked it with bass, walleye, perch, crappies, bluegills, northern pike and told them to grow big and fast. He provided the deer, bear, muskrat, mink, otter, beaver, skunk, porcupine, grouse, ducks, prairie chickens a natural, idyllic habitat.

He made sure the air was crisp and clean, the water pure and cold, and the tranquility broken only by the loon calling. He managed to have it almost inaccessible. Twenty miles from the nearest town on rough, pot-holey county roads, then onto various rutty, one-lane, dirt logging trails that cut through the woods, twist around hillocks, and dip across little creeks. It remains as serene today as it was in the very beginning. The fish are not as big or the stringers as full as they once were except weeks and months later when they naturally grow with the stories that are told.

The one thing He overlooked in putting this whole plan together was the cast of characters that somehow migrated here regularly on a pilgrimage to mix fun with their fishing. It was as if the United Nations and a Funny Farm held conventions here at the same time. What was once almost untouched by human hands now became Knobby's Place.

2  Knobby

he day he was born he let it be known that he repelled his name. His cries were louder, longer, and more often than the other babies. His mother thought it was her milk. The doctor said it was the croup. His father offered no opinion because he had already left for parts unknown. If most people were asked, they would agree that anyone tagged with a name like Garnett Hubert Noblitt deserved to be cranky.

His mother said the reason for naming her first baby Garnett Hubert Noblitt was that she was always fascinated by the reddish-crystal like rock and thought the name had a nice sound regardless whether her baby was a boy or a girl. She added the extra T when she saw his appendage. The name Hubert was that of a teenage sweetheart she once fondled and for whom she would always hold dear to her. The name of the person who helped conceive Garnett Hubert Noblitt could have been most any Tom, Dick, or Harry among the loggers, railroaders, and drifters working their way west for fame and fortune. Melba Lou Noblitt was known as a free loving female who never met a stranger.

The limbs of her branch of the Noblitt family tree were trimmed, pruned, and weathered, and so sketchy they could hardly be traced. And if Melba Lou were ever asked she would probably say she gave poor little Knobby his name in order to get even with those who stuck her with "Melba Lou."

Soon after Garnett was weaned Melba Lou dumped him on the steps of the Episcopal church and headed west with some dandy salesman to find fame and fortune in California. Garnett was soon turned over to a nice middle-aged couple who started calling him Gar. This arrangement lasted but a few years and the couple gave him up because of his mischievous behavior, especially after Gar tried to play Tarzan from their priceless chandeliers and came falling down in a pile of plaster and crystals. That exhibition was by no means the crowning blow but merely one of many exasperating acts that led the nice middle-aged couple, who had aged rapidly, to turn Gar over to another foster home.

The foster home process eventually matriculated Gar to a Foundling and Children's Home and then later to a Boys School. These institutions externally exhibited every good intention but the public cannot appreciate how unrewarding the experiences are for young boys growing up in their puberty years. This was the case with Knobby who by now disliked the name Gar as much as he did his entire moniker. Once he wrestled some kid down to the gymnasium floor, sat on the kid's chest with his fist cocked, and yelled, "You call me 'Knobby' or I'll crack your head." And that was all anyone else needed to be encouraged that from then on it was going to be Knobby or heads would roll.

Knobby was by now acquiring physical features that worked well with the name Knobby. In his late teens he developed stocky, broad, hockey player shoulders, a thick neck, and a face that resembled a Popeye looking potato. With his personal disposition and a physique to match, the other young men didn't mess around with Knobby and the young women didn't have much to do with him either.

He dispatched himself from Boys School early and

hooked up with a railroad crew doing road gang work and moved with the crew as they began building a branch of the railroad to the northern part of the country. He liked this kind of work and the freedom of not being accountable to anyone or anything. He was known as a loner not bothering anyone but having the reputation as a hard worker. Knobby also liked the area in which the crew was now working. The air was crisp. The days long in summer. The surroundings were a blending of rolling, wide open hillsides, and thick pine tree forests. Since he really never knew this kind of environment, he began to respect and appreciate the serenity and solitude. When the railroad crew was moved back south to work on another track line, he stayed.

Lars Severson was a major influence in this area owning the garbage removal and the short haul delivery service companies, and the ever-popular Swedes Saloon in this small town. Knobby worked for Lars for several years. By the time he was in his late twenties Knobby knew all about the garbage and hauling business, knew all the small town politics and personalities, was acquainted with all the prostitutes, and yet he still felt there was something missing in his life.

They say his life really changed after he was made bartender at Swedes. This is when Knobby began to get his nose deeper and deeper into the alcoholic sauce. His hangovers hit him harder. He showed up late for work and quite often still drunk from the night before. Lars tried to talk sense to him but apparently it didn't work. He became belligerent with customers and with some who had befriended him here in town. To be perfectly frank, Knobby was plainly a son of a bitch. What brought all this to an end was the night Lars walked in and found his drunken bartender on the floor sitting on a customer's chest with his fist primed and cocked. That was the last time Knobby ever worked for Lars.

Knobby stumbled out of Swedes Saloon, went to his

boarding room, stuffed a bottle in each of his pockets and headed out to the woods. He wandered out there for several days until Jack the Bum found him stretched over the bank of Stillman's River. Jack thought Knobby was a goner but learned he still had some life in him because he grunted when Jack nudged him with his foot. Jack tugged, carried, pushed, and pulled Knobby to his shack in the woods where Stillman's widens to what some would consider a small lake.

Actually it was Jack the Bum's dog that found Knobby and barked Jack to the spot by the river. Jack's dog was a combination Weimaraner and German Shepherd, gangly as a wet spaghetti noodle with patches of hair on its back looking like it had been shaved with a dull blade. It barked when it wanted attention and snored when it was comfortable. Jack called his dog, Noah because it always brought things back to the shack. In the mornings he would find pretty colored stones, pine cones, driftwood, tin cans, bottles, and other things the dog would mouth up and carry back and dump on the steps.

The next few days Jack and Noah nursed Knobby back on his feet. "Son, you were one sick cookie. You sure were."

"Where the hell am I?" Knobby moaned, and as his vision cleared he recognized Jack the Bum. "Jack, is this your place?"

"Sure is. And you're the first company I've had in a long time."

Well, the two of them hit it off very well. Jack had a small vegetable garden. Knobby enjoyed working it. Jack caught fish in the river, snared rabbits and grouse, had venison put away in his root storage cellar. Knobby enjoyed the diet. He shared Jack's company and his shack for almost a year. Jack's place was a large log and frame house much more than a shack, but everyone said "Jack's Shack" because the words came out that way. There was a large room with stone fireplace, an open kitchen, two bedrooms, an attic storage area, outside toilet, and the root storage cellar Jack had dug into the side of a hill.

It was located on a rise in a clearing about 500 yards from the river, and surrounded by towering evergreens. The only way into Jack's was through a two-mile, former logging trail. Jack had no car and would bushwhack the trail with his axe everytime he needed to go into town which was only when he ran out of supplies and whiskey, and to check his mail for his disability check. Once on the county roads, he could hitch-hike the twenty miles to town. Never failed to get a ride since everybody knew good old Jack the Bum.

Jack had an old wooden boat and the two of them would row on out into the river and fish the day away. It was during these little outings that Jack talked with Knobby about his booze problem, and oddly enough, ever since Knobby was yanked from almost falling in the river he had not touched a drop. And this was in spite of Jack nipping on a bottle every evening.

"This whole place is going to change pretty soon," Jack remarked one day on the river.

"How do you mean?" Knobby replied.

"I hear some company's putting in a dam way down the ways by Little Porcupine," said Jack. "Yes, that will flood the whole countryside up. Trees and all."

Knobby became interested and said, "What about your place? It won't cover that up will it?"

"Man came in here some time ago and told me all about it. Said it would flood over all the rivers and from what they know my place would be safe."

"I bet you're glad to know that," said Knobby.

"Oh, won't make too much difference to me since I don't expect to be around then but you will."

"The hell you say. You'll outlive me, Jack."

The conversation continued like this early in the evening after they had eaten and were sitting on the steps of the shack. Jack the Bum was smoking his pipe and nipping on his bottle. Knobby was whisking his hands over his face trying to ward off the mosquitos. They didn't bother Jack.

"Son, you're only making those mosquitos madder doing that," Jack stated. "You're also working yourself into a tizzy."

Knobby could not stand the hovering mosquitos and was angered that he could not ward them off as Jack did. He watched Jack and saw that all he did was to slowly move his hands to his face whenever they were not occupied with his pipe or bottle.

Knobby sharply said, "The reason they don't go after you is that your beard covers half your face and that tobacco smoke chases them off."

"Nope. You got to have an understanding with mosquitos. If you don't harm them, they won't harm you. But you got to do it gently so they'll understand."

Knobby never did get their complete understanding but he did grow a beard and started smoking a pipe.

"Man said that his company now owns all the land around where the lake will be, but I'm okay."

"That should make you feel good," Knobby replied.

"I'm surprised you didn't hear any of this talk when you were working in town. Lars Severson knows all about it."

"Why, hell yes, he should," snapped Knobby.

Jack smiled between puffs. "Can't touch me. Man said the company found out I had mineral rights, everlasting or something, with the government and I will still own these forty acres."

The two of them continued sitting there in silence until Jack said, "It's all there in the old leather satchel tucked away in the root cellar in case you're interested."

Knobby was curious about his directness but then again it

was also not unlike Jack to ramble.

The next day they went out fishing again and Knobby tried to envision how all the water created from the dam would look as it filled in the valleys. "Son, I'm all petered today," Jack said. "You mind rowing us in." Knobby noticed how drained Jack was looking and how feeble he seemed as he helped Jack from the boat and into the shack. Jack stayed in bed the rest of that day and the next, not eating much and not touching his bottle. When Noah barked outside the following morning Knobby knew Jack was gone.

It was not much of a funeral. Only a few of Jack's oldtime friends helped Knobby bury him back in the woods. After that it wasn't long before Lars came driving up to Jack's shack and asked Knobby how long he planned to stay here. Knobby said he didn't know for sure but what business was it to Lars. "I'm planning to buy this property from Jack Tackett's heirs," was all Lars said then drove back down the narrow path.

Well, Lars never pulled that off. Knobby found the satchel tucked away in the root cellar and read where Jack had left everything to him. The forty acres, the shack, Noah, his boat, everything including being the beneficiary of his government life insurance. In addition to that Jack had accumulated a couple of thousand of dollars in cold cash that was also willed to Knobby. It was all perfectly legal. Knobby had inherited Jack the Bum's estate.

The first thing Knobby did was to buy a pickup truck and widen the narrow two-mile stretch from the county road. He installed inside plumbing. He worked on the garden, cleared some land by the river, and generally got the place straightened up. By now the water was beginning to rise in what was being called Lake of Six Rivers. When Knobby would take the boat down Stillman's River he could see where the water backed up by the dam was starting to inundate more and more acres. In a few more years the flooding was complete and the water level left a beautiful shoreline on what was now his property.

Then, Knobby's life style changed again. Somehow fishermen found his narrow two-mile stretch and would come to ask if they could rent his boat. At first he didn't mind but when more and more of them came he started renting it out by the hour. Knobby was now at a point where he had to make a decision about what to do about getting more boats. He got help making up his mind the day Joseph "Joie Tough" Tufano and his entourage drove the sleek, black, elongated Cadillac into the clearing in front of Knobby's. Four men, strangely and sleekly dressed got out of the car at the same time, looked all around, then "Joie Tough" met nose-to-nose with Knobby and said, "I want to buy your boat." Knobby said they could use it but it was not for sale.

"I wanna buy this place," Joie Tough then claimed. Knobby stood his ground and said it was not for sale either. "You're welcome to use this boat and spend some time inside, but don't talk to me anymore about buying anything." Knobby was getting bristly.

A lot of things could have happened at that initial confrontation. Knobby didn't budge and Joie Tough went back to the car and talked with the others. He came back and told Knobby they wanted to use his boat. The four of them piled in and warily rowed out into the waters of Lake of Six Rivers. About three hours later they returned still sitting in the same cautious position from where they started.

"What you call your place?" Joie Tough asked.

"I don't call it anything," replied Knobby.

"What you called?" Joie Tough asked.

"I'm known as Knobby."

"Okay, Knobby. Here's some bucks. I'd like you to put up a cabin for me on that point there. Get some more boats. Put up a couple more cabins in the woods for my friends. Fix this

place up a little. Put in a lounge where we can drink and eat. Nothing fancy but you got the makings here for a nice place for a lot of nice people I know. And I'll make it right for you right down the line. Whatta ya say, Knobby?"

Knobby felt the large roll of bills being forced into both his hands and sensed he had little choice except to say, "Why don't we go inside and talk it over."

They talked and contrary to what people would have thought Knobby agreed to go ahead and make this into a small fishing camp where Tufano and his friends could come a couple of times during the year to get away from things. Tufano agreed and encouraged Knobby to have others use the cabins when he wasn't. Joie Tough said, "I've done some checking and this place will be the only fishing camp on the whole lake. No problem."

Knobby could now imagine the commercial venture that was being proposed when his thoughts were interrupted by, "And dat Lars guy will never be able to touch this place." Knobby appeared dumbfounded by his remark and before he could ask Tufano said, "We've already handled that problem."

They sealed the agreement with a handshake and a hug-kiss from Joseph Tufano. He looked Knobby in the eye and said, "From now on, partner, this is Knobby's Place."

With that the foursome entered the Cadillac and drove out down the narrow two-mile stretch of dirt road.

It took a few days for Knobby to realize what he had agreed to but in the months ahead a cabin was constructed on the point of land by the shore where Joie Tough wanted it. Knobby called it Breezy Point. Then in the years following more cabins went up: Whispering Pines, Cedar Rest, Hillside, Lakeview, Tuckaway, Lake Haven, Northern Air, and other exotic vacation type names. Boats and motors were available. The lounge was finished and became the socializing center for those staying at the camp as well as for the natives in the area who would gather here on Friday and Saturday nights.

In spite of all this commercial expansion the setting still retained its solitude being surrounded by towering evergreens and huge hardwoods. And, as Joie Tough said, it was the only camp throughout the entire body of water. The fishing was outstanding. The peace and quiet overpowering. Jack the Bum would have been surprised at the changes but would have enjoyed seeing and talking with all the characters who now came here to enjoy their fishing vacation at Knobby's Place.

3 | Ralph LeBlanc, Guide Extraordinaire

The way the lake system was naturally arranged the likelihood of anyone becoming totally lost was very remote. Oh, sure, there were one or two situations in earlier years where fishermen would go as far as they could into the backwaters and become disoriented, but when patience prevailed they could always find their way back into the main body of water. Knobby, and others as well, made it a point around dusk to discreetly check to see if all the boats were in and they usually had a good idea when and if to suspect a problem. On those occasions someone would head on out looking for the fishermen and would invariably find them either rowing back because the motor conked out or waiting it out on some island for help to arrive.

Only once can anyone recall a couple of fishermen spending the night in the woods. But they did it by design wanting to "rough it" they said. Knobby told them a thing or two about that stunt.

First timers could readily become frustrated with the many islands dotting the water, and the fact that the shoreline looked the same all over. But once people got the lay of the land, directions were no problem. Knobby, of course, knew the layout like the back of his hand and you could always count on him for help on things to watch for and places to fish. This could not be said of some of the others who were quite specific with their directions although far less accurate. "Where didja catch that string of fish?" a new group would ask. The response would be, "In the upper lip!" And after a while those newly initiated neophytes would respond to a similar question with, "At my favorite hole." So you could tell very quickly the directions were explicit yet interpretive.

In the event anyone, however, really wanted to know the where, when, how, what of catching fish all they had to do was sidle up to old Raul LeBlanc, the unofficial, unauthorized, and obtrusive guide of these parts. A beer or two or three would also loosen the old codger and he would be overly willing to relate his wisdom of these waters.

There really was no need to hire a guide here but Ralph, as he was more commonly called, took fancy to the title and the self-established authority that appeared to come with it. Although Knobby never encouraged the guests to use Ralph as their guide, he never discouraged it either. Knobby felt it would be a heckuva experience for anyone to use Ralph but he didn't want to be part of the prodding. It would always be some of the old time regulars that would encourage and excite some of the new fishermen to use Ralph. They would say that if they were only here for a short time and wanted to catch some fish and relish the succulence of a shore lunch in the wilderness, then they should have Ralph guide them.

Raul LeBlanc was a French-Canadian kind of resident that wandered into this area years ago. He claims to have been a one-time trapper, logger, miner, railroader, farmer but you really never knew too much about him. You could depend that he would always be around. Camp handyman picking up garbage, chopping wood, dipping out minnows, handling the gas and oil, cleaning boats, fixing cabins, taking care of the fish shack. These part-time chores left him little time to pursue his guiding profession but offered him little interference to his full-time avocation of boozing. He did this extremely well, so well that only those who closely knew him and his consumption level could tell when Ralph was tipsy. His preference was brandy and a beer chaser but mostly he drank a lot of beer. It showed up by the pot he carried around the size forty waist which was the mid-point of a lean 170 pound torso supported by spindly, but strong legs below. Ralph smelled of soiled clothes and stale beer. He had a full head of salt and pepper colored hair and a bronze, weathered face from being outside for sixty some years. Very seldom did he remove the worn baseball-type cap with the word "Remington" on the front, but when he did you could notice his lighter complexioned forehead. Some close friends called him "One Quart Low."

He lived way back in the woods in a small tarpaper shanty for as long as anyone can remember. His place had a wood stove, hot plate, bed, and stuffed chair which swallowed Ralph when he sat in it. He used a kerosene lamp mostly so he wouldn't over-tax the 40 watt bulbs he used in a few other lamps. There was a small wash basin in what he called his kitchen. His own private toilet was thirty yards away out in back. You found his place by taking the well worn path leading for three quarters of a mile from camp.

Ralph was probably fairly good as a guide but his biggest problem was that he usually had a hangover most mornings. It was hard to tell but he would hurt. One of his tricks when he went out guiding would be to fill a coffee can with ice which he placed next to him as he ran the boat. He would take his knife, chip off some ice, and suck on it. By noon the ice would be gone and Ralph ready for another round of belly-warming brandy and beer.

He could make things very exasperating for Knobby yet nothing much ever came from his "mis-adventures." Like the one morning he took two fishermen out at dawn for crappies. Ralph, still woozy from the night before, took them up river to where the dead trees still stood tall in the water. They hit it just right and within a couple of hours they had enough crappies to feed the camp. On the way back Ralph ran over a submerged stump and sheared the pin. Not overly organized, he had no spare pin so took to the oars attempting to row all the way back. He smiled broadly and said, "If it weren't for bad luck I'd have no luck at all," and with that sure enough along came another boat. Luckily, Ralph got a shear pin, fixed the motor, and they were back at camp by noon.

Funny thing about all this was later when Ralph was unloading the boat he looked over at the next boat pulled up on shore. It was then he realized that in the early morning dim, and through unfocused eyes, he had taken the wrong boat. Just then a couple of fishermen came out of their cabin and asked, "You getting things cleaned up for us, Ralph?"

"Yeah, just checking to be sure you got enough gas. Did you know you didn't have a shear pin taped to the motor handle? I'll bring one down for you before you go out."

When the two left for home they mentioned to Knobby how thoughtful Ralph was. Yes, old Ralph would come out "smelling like a rose" every time.

Two of the oddest looking characters considering themselves fishermen hired Ralph one day to guide them for walleyes and to prepare shore lunch. They had heard how delicious shore lunch could be when done by gourmet Ralph. Now these two guys looked like something right out of a sporting goods catalog. Both wore identical attire except one

was all in tan and the other a pale green. Twill pants crisply pressed. Rubber soled, leather top moccasins. Safari-type shirts with the collar buttoned. Floppy canvas hats with all kinds of flies stuck in them. Each had the same dime-store type spin casting outfit. One still had the staple caught on one of the guides, and the price tag was still stuck on the handle of the other rod. You could imagine what the talk was around camp when they saw these two arrive.

The walleyes were not hitting very well that morning and they had only three just-barely keepers by lunch time.

"We have enough sustenance for shore lunch, don't we, Raul?" asked one of them.

"Sustenance your ass," Ralph muttered, but loudly said, "Well, we'll have to make do 'cause they sure ain't hitting this morning."

"Oh, that should be just fine," the other chirped.

Ralph unpacked the lunch provisions while the two

walked arm-in-arm along the shore and on into the woods. "Those twits," he said then exclaimed, "Great balls of fire! I forgot the stove." Ralph not only forgot to pack the propane stove but he went out without any matches. He had beans, corn, potatoes, bread, butter, jelly, corn meal, lard, and three small walleyes but no fire. He filleted the walleyes cleanly, sprinkled corn meal over them slightly and pressed them into two sandwiches. Opened the cans of beans and corn, sliced the potatoes, and spread all this out on some flat pieces of driftwood.

"Hey, you two. Lunch is ready."

Ralph consumed the three cans of beer he had stashed away while the other two hungrily gulped down the lunch.

"Our compliments to the chef," said the one outfitted in tan. "That was a most unusual meal."

"Excellent cuisine, my friend," said the pale green outfit.

"Coseene, your ass," Ralph coughed under his breath.

Later in the day those two brand new fishing outfits brought in a nice string of walleyes. Knobby met them as they pulled up on shore at camp.

"We had a most rewarding experience. And your man, Raul, was utterly masterful with his culinary selection."

With that the one in tan handed Ralph a twenty dollar bill. Knobby stood open-mouthed as the two of them walked off. "What the hell did you do?" he asked Ralph.

Ralph merely muttered, "Those twits!"

Ralph came very close one year to taking the cure and abstaining once and for all from alcohol, and anyone with a frailer fortitude would probably have done so. It was early spring and many of the natives in the area were chomping at the bit to open the fishing season. Ice had gone out of the water completely but there was still a chilly nip in the air. During the winter Knobby always shut off the water in the cabins, and since the lines were not set too deep in the ground, he turned the water on only when there was more consistent warm weather. The cabins were usable with a small wood-burning stove throwing out enough concentrated heat to generally warm the occupants, but water for cooking, dishes, washing, and flushing the toilet had to be brought in from the lake if someone wanted to use a cabin early in the year. That's when there would be several large milk cans filled with lake water and sitting inside by the door. When a can or two went dry, they were taken to the lake, filled and brought back inside the cabin.

As had been custom for years five of Ralph's friends planned to spend that opening day weekend in one of the cabins with Ralph joining them. What a crew this was! Their agenda was primarily party time, laughs, cards, booze, and lots of stories. The group consisted of: Jailer John, the local constable who had a knack of turning the other cheek; Doctor DuCette who drove over 200 miles to be at this occasion; Fibber Farquahar, you could bet he would get the biggest fish; Tonto Tom O'Brien, your basic half-Irish half-Sioux Indian; Little Joe Rosselli who at one time played semi-pro football and once kicked a ball so hard it exploded. Then there was Ralph whose main job was to get the grocery and liquor supply, open up the cabin, get things set up, and greet the guys when they arrived.

They all showed up pretty much on time, luckily for Ralph who had started his brandy and beer regime earlier in the day. It wasn't long before the six of them had a glow on in the cabin. Tale after tale was told far into the night until the effects of the alcohol did them in and they literally dropped to sleep wherever they may have had their last swallow.

Little Joe was the first to get up the next morning and with a hangover to end them all. The others were still completely absorbed in sleep. He relieved his bladder and carried in one of the milk cans of water to flush the toilet. Little Joe

didn't realize he had taken the can in which Ralph had put several dozen minnows so they wouldn't freeze outside. He poured the water down the bowl and went back to sleep. Shortly, Ralph was the next to use the toilet. He also had a head as painful as Little Joe's. Ralph steadied himself over the toilet bowl, began to piss, them saw the school of minnows thrashing in the water. "Oh, great balls of fire! The devil's got me for sure. I've got the DT's," Ralph sputtered.

He looked up at the ceiling and slobberly but solemnly exclaimed, "No more drinkin' for me." He then tried to drown his dryness with a cup of water taken from the can Little Joe had brought in. Ralph took a deep mouthful, started choking, then spewed out water all over the place. On the floor squirmed a silvery minnow. "Oh, great balls of fire! Now I've got'em inside me."

The following night the group was at it again including Ralph and all his threats of abstention. This time the minnows remained outside regardless of how cold it was.

4 Sam the Chumming Man

One thing you can be sure of whenever you fish at one specific camp or location for any length of time is that you are bound to meet and become acquainted with a character or two, and most often more. Fishing has a natural way of bringing out hidden inhibitions. It's a matter of letting one's hair down. Look at all the fishermen that dress themselves in military fatigues, camouflaged outfits. You would think they were stalking and ready to ambush an enemy far more formidable than the piscatorial prey. Some astute angler once said, "Fishing is the excuse to be something other than what people think you are in your day-to-day environment."

Well, Knobby's certainly had its share of excuses. One of them was Sam the Chumming Man. More officially he was Sam Ackermann, a diverse combination of personalities only a mother could appreciate. But in Sam's situation there were strong doubts even about that conviction.

Sam was in his late sixties, thin as a rail but tough as nails. Actually, he looked like he was in a constant state of malnutrition. Many believed he purposely appeared to be on the brink of starvation so that he could sponge meals from others in the camp. He did right well in this respect since there was hardly an evening meal he didn't eat at somebody else's cabin.

Knobby told him he should drink muddy water so he would make a shadow. Sam would scoff and reply naively that he drank plenty of coffee and that should be enough to make his shadow.

As thin and tough as he was, he was also as tight as a mouse's ear. And to make matters even more complex, Sam was almost stone deaf. You could say some disparaging things about him and his behavior and not hurt his feelings, except there were times when Sam heard what he wanted to hear. He had a way of turning up his hearing aids and heard very well. Like the time Moose Weinantz, the used car dealer, was telling the group that had settled in at Knobby's Lounge about how cheap Sam was. "That ol' codger's never bought a round in all the years he's come here," Moose stated.

"What the hell!" Sam blurted out, startling Moose and his group of listeners. Sam always prefaced most of his limited oration with "What the hell!"

"Don't give me the business about being cheap," Sam continued. "You're the guy that's cheap. You walked out of DeeDee's the other night without paying. Who the hell you think you are talking about?" (The comment about DeeDee's will be clarified later).

Moose turned an uncomfortable blush and said, "Sam, I didn't mean 'cheap' like in tight or stingy. I mean 'cheap' like in frugal or economical. You know, like cautious with your money." Now doesn't that sound like something a used car dealer would say?

Sam heard all of this loud and clear. He got up from his chair and walked to the bar. He pulled out a roll of bills from his pocket that looked about the size of a Tampax for an elephant. He handed two twenty dollar bills to Ralph who was tending bar and said, "Give those guys a drink over there and make sure that melon head Moose gets a double." And although talking loud came natural for Sam, he went a pitch higher and belted out, "Ralph, you make sure DeeDee gets one of those twenties and tell her I'm paying for Moose's tart the other night."

With that Sam stormed outside and headed down the path toward his cabin, Cedar Rest. As he walked he turned on his all-powerful flashlight and looked into every garbage can along the way. Any anger he had was short-lived as he found a nice large plastic bleach bottle. He was too far away, of course, to be tuned in to the comment Moose made, "See, I told you it would work."

The Ackermann family was one of the largest junk dealers in the midwest. Well known, respected, shrewd business people who had amassed a small fortune. Sam was the oldest of four brothers and two sisters. A basic traditionalist he was the least inclined to change even to the point of being plain cantankerous. Sam knew the junk business but he lacked the finesse and charm the rest of the family possessed. Sam was different and became much more so after a load of junk fell on him while he was squeezed under the dashboard of a wrecked car trying to remove one of the instrument gauges. Nothing escaped Sam. The official report was that the magnet became disconnected and a load of scrap iron came clattering down right on top of that car. The investigation was brief and concluded the accident was a matter of fate. After the noise and dust settled, the first words that were heard were, "What the hell!" and Sam squirmed out from under that mess with only minor cuts and bruises, and hard of hearing from then on.

It wasn't long afterwards that the family bought out his interest in the business which left Sam more than a pretty penny. At least a million to be more exact. Well, the first thing he did was to buy a Checker cab and have the back seat removed. The next thing he did was get married. Not once, but twice. The first lasted six months. This wife walked out with a couple thousand dollars she found stashed away in one of Sam's shoe boxes. Fortunately for Sam, she didn't check his socks where he concealed several more thousands. The second wife was a friend of the first, unbeknownst to Sam, and she lived with him for about a year. It was Sam who wanted out of this marriage because, as he said, she didn't talk loud enough. She would mouth her words and Sam would have to turn up his hearing aids until the buzzing would drive him nuts. "What the hell! Talk up, will ya. I can't hear a damn thing you're saying."

You can imagine how that must have appeared whenever the two of them went out in public which was something this second wife wanted to do often. If the truth were known, this bride purposely talked in low tones and would pretend to say something only the words never came out.

It was after the second divorce that Sam started coming up to Knobby's. At first for a week or two at a time. Then it was six months from May through October. Knobby set him up in the Cedar Rest cabin because it had a large front porch arrangement for his many supplies and was tucked away in the woods.

Sam would drive his Checker cab into camp pulling his fishing boat. It looked more like he was pulling a pregnant whale. If lucky, Sam unloaded his caravan in half a day. He might have been better off hiring a Mayflower mover to make the trip. First, he removed all the items from the back of the cab where the rear seat had been removed. Then the trunk of the cab, then the boat. Sam carried in minnow buckets, worm boxes, coolers, ice chests, fuel tanks, anchors, depth finders, battery chargers, tackle boxes, rods, reels, metal detectors, marker buoys, and boxes and boxes of empty plastic bottles. He had at least two of everything and usually more than that.

Sam believed in quantity discounts. After he unloaded, the front porch at Cedar Rest looked like a warehouse with all the gear piled high. And everything had to be stacked in a certain way so Sam would know if anything had been touched. Those who had nothing to do the day Sam arrived stood in awe watching him unload. Most of the stuff was brand new. He usually replaced everything before he came up for the season.

Nobody volunteered to help. They knew better since Sam wanted it this way. Nobody even bothered to help him get his boat in the water because this was a show in itself, and nobody wanted to miss it. You can imagine that awkward looking Checker cab backing down the sandy launching beach. It appeared as if it would slither down to its fenders, but Sam was so deft at launching, the rear wheels never even touched the water. A couple of quick jerks and the boat would roll off the trailer. Sam held on to the long rope while parking the Checker cab, then pulled the boat on shore.

The Checker cab was Sam's pride and joy. When he wasn't out fishing or looking in garbage cans, he was cleaning the cab. Carmie Calabrese from the Italian Connection would wander over occasionally to see what kind of polish Sam used.

Regardless of Sam's idiosyncrasies, he was an exceptionally good fisherman, and also made no bones telling everyone about his ability. One look at all the fish mounts on the walls in Knobby's Lounge indicated that half of them belonged to Sam. He took perch, bluegill, walleye, crappie, bass, northern pike back to a taxidermist he knew and had them mounted, then he brought them back with him the following season and nailed them to the walls. Knobby could have put a stop to this but since Sam was paying for the taxidermy work this kind of exhibit helped to encourage the fishing business.

One spring Sam returned with a very unusual mount. Upon arrival he went directly to the lounge and unveiled a beautiful striped bass that weighed 28 pounds and was 38 inches long. It was a striking mount against a glistening grain walnut board. All the measurements were inscribed on a small brass plate along with the heading "Sam Ackermann. Caught August 1969." Knobby and the others in the lounge seeing this shook their heads in disbelief. "What the hell!" was Sam's only response.

Overlooking the source of that striper, Sam caught more fish than most people here. He had several secrets for his success. One of them was to mark the spots where he caught fish with those plastic bottles he brought up. That's why he had an abundant supply and was always looking for more by rummaging through the garbage cans. It was nothing to see twenty or more plastic bottles floating on the water. "That's where Sam the Chummer fishes," people would say as they spotted the bottles. Then they would anchor around the perimeter expecting to fill their stringers with fish.

Only Sam was smarter than his hard of hearing let on. He would slip out very early in the morning and drop those floating markers in places where dynamite couldn't raise a fish. He did this in two or three spots, then took off for his favorite haunts where he also planted a few bottles, enough to throw off visitors. And people wondered why his spots didn't produce fish like they did for Sam.

Once in a while the trick backfired on him as it did one day when Little Joe spied him in a secluded bay with his stringer down in the water. Sam was having a nice run on the walleyes here. So Little Joe sneaked out very early the next morning before Sam went out to fish. He pulled up all of Sam's markers from a previous spot and dropped them in this bay where Sam had his run the day before. Since there were so many markers now scattered all over this place, Sam completely by-passed the bay when he went out later. He saw Little Joe parked among all those markers and believed it was one of his false spots. He smiled deviously as he motored by.

So did Little Joe.

How Sam was nicknamed "The Chummer" was the result of another of his little secrets. Sometimes during a rain or just afterwards you would see Sam out looking for worms. You would also see him at night with his flashlight looking for nightcrawlers. Now you know why he brought up all those worm boxes. And why he gathered up all the newspapers in camp so he could shred them for his worms. That's why he threw all his coffee grounds out behind his cabin so he could dig for worms. Sam took an ample amount of worms out with him everytime he went fishing. The first thing he would do is fling handfuls and handfuls of worms out on the water. Then, he would bait up with worms waiting for the fish to bite. And it worked.

If he didn't use worms for chumming, he used minnows. Whenever groups left camp and had minnows left you could bet Sam would cabbage on to them. That's why Sam had so many minnow buckets among his assortment of fishing gear. In addition to getting minnows from others, you could find Sam wading small creeks out in the woods netting for minnows. You would also see him wading stealthily along the shore. Sam used the same technique with minnows as he did with the worms. Once he stopped at a spot, out would go dipperfuls of minnows. And this worked also.

It appeared one day as if Sam the Chumming Man would give up on minnows for his chumming. He had been out most of the day and exhausted his worm supply. He pulled up to a spot where the lake system spilled out into a stream that connected to another part of the overall lake. Sam thought this would be an ideal place to chum with minnows. He chummed out about five dozen, almost all he had in the minnow buckets. Most of them floated and were caught up in the current, others swam for the current. Seeing all these minnows going to waste, every sea gull in the area swooped down for those

minnows. Hawking, squawking, fighting, scrapping they came
darting in over Sam. Even the crows mixed in and competed
with the gulls. As deaf as he was Sam heard all this commotion and swatted at them like he did with mosquitos until he
was able to get the boat off and heading back to camp. The
birds always recognized Sam and whenever he chummed with
minnows down they descended on him.

Sam and Ralph LeBlanc were fairly close to one another.
Sam liked to visit Ralph because he always thought he would
find some treasure along the path leading to Ralph's tarpaper
shanty. And Ralph liked to see Sam visit because he always
could count on him bringing a gallon of burgundy wine. The
two of them would sit in almost darkness at Ralph's shanty
sipping from that wine jug.

"What the hell! When you going to get some lights here?"

"Can't see worth a crap anyhow. Why should I have more lights?"

"Whattya say?"

"Got no money," Ralph yelled and followed softly saying, "You thin turd."

"I heard that," hollered Sam.

The two of them would sit there in semi darkness chatting about their past, their appetites, their aches and pains. Ralph always wondered why he had a sore throat the morning following one of Sam's visits.

"You keep drinkin' that stuff, Ralph, and you'll have lead in your pencil."

Ralph yelled back, "But I don't have anyone to write to." Then the two of them would laugh together until they quietly became still and sat rocking gently in their chairs. You barely could see Ralph sitting in his large stuffed chair.

"What the hell! Been to DeeDee's lately?"

"No. Haven't, Sam. You?"

"Not for a while. How 'bout you?"

"You ol' Chum Head. You can't hear worth a shit! I just told ya', No."

"That reminds me of a joke," said Sam. "Ralph, you hear about the old man who was on a television quiz show and they asked him how often he had sex."

"I don't have a television."

"Whattya say?"

"No. I didn't hear about the guy."

"Well, the old man told them he had sex once a year. Then the TV guy asked him why he was smiling so much." Sam stopped and said nothing. Ralph raised slightly from his stuffed chair, gulped a swallow of wine and said, "What's the joke, Sam?"

"Whattya say?"

"I said is that the end of the story?"

"What the hell! No, it's not the end. The old man that was smiling said, 'tonight's the night!' Got it? How often he had sex. Tonight's the night!"

Ralph let his chair swallow him. He had some more wine then said resignedly, "That's no joke. It's more like the god-damn truth."

When Sam wasn't fishing or cleaning his cab he would be looking for things. You would see him walking around the cabins with his metal detector buzzing because he had to have it set on high. All he ever found was nails, bottle caps, odds and ends like that, but whenever he found a coin whatever the denomination you would think it was right out of Ft. Knox. Sam would walk along the shore picking up rocks, driftwood, rusty lures. He was never still, always on the go. Knobby said it was because he never hears much of what's going on.

Sam's get-up-and-go almost came to a halt one night after he was slowly returning from a visit to Ralph's. Sam and his flashlight shakily were picking their way along the path back to their cabin. He knew whenever he left the path because he would stumble into a tree. Then his loud voice would penetrate the wooded quiet. "What the hell!"

As Sam neared the camping area his flashlight spotted a garbage can. Sam didn't think he had rummaged through this one in a while so he marched right over to it and pointed that flashlight into the assortment of stuff. Sam never heard the fury masked animal that clawed, scratched, and bolted from the garbage. He never even saw it as it shot out, knocked over the garbage can, sent Sam falling backwards, then waddled as fast as it could into the woods.

Sam the Chumming Man lay there passed out in a heap of beer bottles, coffee grounds, potato peelings, fish bones, scraps of all kinds. The flashlight lay beside him beaming to

ward the cabins. Some minutes later a man came out of one of the cabins and while taking a leak saw the flashlight beam. He got the rest of his group and they came to the garbage heap where they found Sam. They brushed him off and helped him back to Cedar Rest.

"Sam, you okay?" one of them asked.

"What the hell!" he responded.

Old Sam the Chummer certainly ranks among the top as one of the major characters at Knobby's. And although he often got a lot of verbal abuse, some of which he heard and some of which he refused to hear, he was always missed when he headed home after his fishing season.

Knobby would always say watching the Checker cab pull away, "There's a bright spot to all this. There's only one of him."

5 The Happy Hour Bunch

It was leaning toward late afternoon in what had been a beautiful day. Cool. Crisp. Bright sun, not a cloud in the sapphire sky. Only a slight ripple on the water from a lazy west wind. Typically, the heart of high pressure weather. Like a lot of perfect weather-wise days the fishing was lousy.

The Happy Hour Bunch gave up on the fishing and headed in after soaking up the sun for most of the day. Anyone on the water knowing these guys could tell approximately what time it was because they always started coming in around 5:00 PM just when a lot of the others were going out. Someone in this Bunch would say, "The sun is on the yardarm and it's happy hour time." The three of them were a fun-loving group very close to each other, having fished together for over twenty-five years. They were quite knowledgeable and skilled in the art of angling, although occasionally their technique and strategy went awry. Actually, if the truth were known they used fishing as a means of solidifying the chemistry of their long-standing friendship.

"We've got about a half dozen or so minnies left. Let's use them up around this sandbar." This was Charlie Winston, the conservative one, suggesting that they make a couple more passes in a fairly shallow stretch before heading in.

"We don't want to miss happy hour," grinned KJ, the raw boned senior member of the group. He was the philosopher, always rationalizing any situation.

"Here's a king-size chub, Brockie. Put this on and we'll troll in this area," directed Charlie who was handling the motor that day.

George Brockman was willing to try anything. He was the entrepreneur. By the end of their fishing trip Brockie, as he was commonly called, would have used every available lure from the "Fibber McGee Closet" he called a tackle box. He would cast, jig, troll, drift, still fish—anything short of dynamiting in his anxiety to hook something. Often he considered using the later. Brockie was quite dexterous being equally accurate at casting with either hand. He could drop a lure on a leaf at fifty paces. Whenever Brockie screwed things up, however, you could always count on old KJ to offer very direct advice and walking-around wisdom. Then Charlie would follow up with his own brand of needling. But Brockie had grown accustomed to these barbs and countered with dry retorts that made the group's repartee a continuous conversational gem.

Brockie fitted a number four hook through the lips of a seven inch sucker minnow and cast it out into the now calm water between two sand spits in the channel. *Plop*.

"That's enough to wake up the dead," said KJ.

"Okay, I'm going to troll around this sandy area, so let's work hard before we go in," said Charlie acting like the proverbial guide. "Plop. Plop. Fizz. Fizz. Oh, what fun it is," crooned KJ. "I sure hope we don't miss happy hour."

They trolled slowly close to shore then out into deeper water, raising and lowering their rods every so often to stimulate more action from the minnow. Within a half hour they covered most of the area.

"We can't seem to raise a thing today," said Charlie.

"That's the way it is with old fishermen," remarked KJ. "Let's head 'er in for happy hour."

The only one who had not reeled in was Brockie who was fussing with his spin casting reel. "This damn reel has never worked right. Can't seem to get the drag set and now the cap is loose."

"How many times have we heard that story?" KJ said slyly. To which Charlie added, "How many times have you said you were gonna get it fixed before the next trip."

All of a sudden Brockie's rod tip bent down into the water. Instinctively, he grabbed the rod and pulled it hard up to his shoulder. The line zinged out until the water opened with a loud explosion. Up and out of it wiggled the nicest smallmouth you could imagine. A first guess put it in the four to five pound class. It would get bigger during happy hour.

"My God! What have I got here?" exclaimed Brockie. The smallmouth darted here and there, in and out of the water until it made a bee-line for their boat. "What the hell am I gonna do now?"

Down under the boat it went and splashed out on the other side. Brockie now had his rod in the water trying to contain that fish. It made a reverse swing to the other side of the boat where it originally hit. Out went more of Brockie's line.

"I can't get this drag set."

"Well, get your rod out of the water and hold it high to get some pressure on the line," barked Charlie. KJ merely reflected over the matter, "You're doing fine, George."

And with that observation the cap loosened from George

Brockman's reel and clanged against the first eyelet on his rod. The line continued to go with the smallmouth, and to make matters worse now Brockie couldn't even turn the reel handle. "Oh, shit."

The smallmouth had enough of this fiasco and off it went in one final pass that broke the extra taut line. Brockie just sat there, shoulders slumped and rod resting on the gunnel. "Oh shit!" was all he could say. It took KJ to relieve the tension. "You did fine, George. Remember, the good Lord puts an oasis of comfort in every desert of calamity. Now let's have happy hour."

"Oh shit!"

This episode was more or less *fait accompli* with the Happy Hour Bunch. They had been coming to Knobby's for many, many years and invariably something would happen, like losing this fish, that would be enough to make most people cry. This group, however, shook it off and considered them as growing experiences. They would stay for a week at a time and always got the cabin called, "Hillside." During their stays they had added certain accoutrements to the place like the ice crusher for their martinis, the outside thermometer, the wine cooler, the rain gauge, the boot cleaner, the Happy Hour plaque—all the important necessities.

It was not unusual for them to drive the forty miles round trip to town at least three times during their stay for refills to their liquid needs. They claimed it was to replenish their first aid kit. On many of these trips they still felt the effects of the night before like what KJ did one time. In the center of town was a locomotive that served as sort of a monument to the bygone days when logging and mining had made the place a boomtown. These industries had since dried up and the town was withering. Residents paid little attention to this iron monster, but at the same time they didn't want it desecrated by drunks.

Well, as Charlie and Brockie went to the liquor store KJ decided he was going to take a walk to clear his head. When the two of them came out of the liquor store KJ was not to be found until they heard his voice shouting, "Toot. Toot" There was KJ in the cab of that locomotive yelling at the top of his voice, "Clear the tracks. I'm coming through."

Some of the townspeople near the square didn't take this demonstration too kindly and took off looking for Jailer John.

"Get you ass down from there. You'll get us all locked up?" KJ stumbled down from the cab.

"Leave you alone for five minutes and you find trouble."

The two of them quickly steered KJ into their car before retribution was delivered. "What the hell you think you were doing?" asked Brockie.

KJ was spread out on the back seat and with a wide smile said, "I always wanted to see what it would be like to run the railroad."

Kenneth (KJ) Jackson was a composite of Gary Cooper, John Wayne, and Henry Fonda all wrapped up in one. He thoroughly enjoyed his retirement years from coaching high school football. He was big boned, rugged and still in the best of shape. Fishing to KJ was therapy and helped to ease many of the pressures he had accumulated as the small town football star turned coach. Throughout those many years he became recognized more as a teacher than a coach, and it was his basic simple approach to life that helped mold teenagers into young men, and they never forgot his lessons. KJ looked at fishing as a way to appreciate the simple raw beauty in the world. A happy hour or two also helped.

George (Brockie) Brockman had made a small fortune right after World War II when he bought into a lumber yard just as the housing business started mushrooming. He had grown up with KJ but it wasn't until the last few years did they become much closer friends. From the lumber business

Brockie ventured into real estate and again at just the right time. Now he had more time to do as he pleased when he pleased. He was the one of the group that really had fishing finesse in spite of an awkward moment or two once in awhile. He really worked hard and diligently at fishing, and he also made sure he looked the part. Every day he appeared wearing a new wardrobe. He was L.L. Bean from his pork pie hat to his rubber bottom boots. Throw in a little Orvis, Woolrich, and Pendleton here and there, and you had the well dressed fisherman. He also leaned a little on the macho side and occasionally he carried a sheath knife strapped to his web belt.

The third member of the Happy Hour Bunch was Charlie Winston. He was always in the mood for a fishing trip and he could get by with it since his small advertising agency in the town where they lived could open and close at his whim. Charlie was the overly organized type. Everything in order. And at the end of the day he'd bring that official-looking tackle box into the cabin so he could rearrange everything into its proper place. He also had his tackle matched, no odds and ends. If the specifications for a seven-foot Shakespeare spinning rod called for using an ultra-light Shakespeare spinning reel, you could bet Charlie would have that. He was so organized that if the instructions recommended using no more than 5/8 ounce lures, that was his limit. No more nor less.

Charlie was also overly in control or at least he tried to be and thought he was. He planned the trips, made out the checklist and rechecked it, delegated who was to do what and when, where the Happy Hour Bunch would fish and how. Although younger than the other two, they tolerated his planning and even welcomed it. But through the years you could see his attention to details starting to slip. The example well remembered by those in camp at the time was when Charlie and KJ took off at dawn one morning after northerns.

What happened was the day before the Happy Hour Bunch arrived a group already in camp came in with a fifteen pound northern, but the talk around the bar was more about the monster they lost in the stumps near Popple Bay. The Happy Hour Bunch arrived in camp late afternoon and heard the convincing story about a trophy size northern that was too tough to catch. This was enough to stir Charlie's juices and spur his imagination to greater heights. He had always dreamed of catching a twenty pound northern. Always talked about it on every trip, but never came close.

They unpacked in a hurry after hearing the tale about the monster. Contrary to his orderliness, Charlie unpacked and had his stuff piled everywhere. He was a bundle of nervous energy and, as usual, tried to take charge. As soon as he rigged up his tackle, out he went to find the boat they were to use. Then he mounted Brockie's fifteen horse motor all by himself. He was ready to go right then and there, but wiser heads prevailed, and he conceded when KJ and Brockie raised the Happy Hour flag outside their cabin.

"Hell, no. We're not going out now," said KJ. "It's time for happy hour. That dumb fish and all the rest can wait 'til tomorrow, then we'll go after it full bore," commented KJ exerting his seniority.

Well, that particular happy hour was extra long, extra potent, and extra relaxing as all three of them konked out quickly that night. The long ride and the anticipation of tomorrow stimulated the effects of their gin martinis. But in spite of their heavy heads Charlie and KJ were up very early the next day and went out in the misty morning to troll for that big northern in Popple Bay. And this was before breakfast, almost an unpardonable sin for this group. Brockie was smart and slept in.

Charlie quickly had the fifteen horse loudly kicking up a good wake, heading for the stumps protecting the bay. KJ

stretched out in the front of the boat and was taking in deep gulps of cool air to clear his head. "You know where you're going?" he asked.

"You bet your ass I do. 'Member that bay with all the sticks in it? We caught some northerns there one time. That's gotta be Popple Bay."

"Know how to get there?"

"Hell, yeah," quipped Charlie, his pulse rate rising over the possibilities of catching that ever-evasive twenty pound northern he had set his sights on for many years.

"You know there are lotsa stumps in there and the water level's down, and I can't see shit," barked KJ turning to see where they were heading. Charlie sashayed the boat between a row of stumps and then gunned the motor hard so the boat would reach the bay at a point where he could shut it off in order to glide in quietly.

Then it happened. The jolt virtually raised KJ a foot above the front seat. When he came down his butt was in the bottom of the boat and his legs draped over the middle seat. It was a miracle he wasn't propelled clean out of the boat. Charlie had been pitched forward and it actually looked as if they had almost exchanged places. Their rods, tackle, oars, minnow bucket, crawlers, leeches, cushions—everything was all over the boat.

"What in the hell did you do now?"

"My God. I must have hit something."

"You sure as hell did," said KJ raising himself from that back-breaking position. "And unless my vision has been impaired from all that gin we've been drinking, we've lost the motor."

"Oh, my God. Brockie will have a fit. How the hell did it come off?"

"Well, from where I sit," said KJ, "it looks as if you didn't have it clamped on tight and it jumped loose when we hit that stump."

"Oh, my God. We've got to find that motor."

"Now just how the bloody hell do you propose we go about doing that?"

After hitting the submerged stump the boat had turned a complete circle and was now facing in the general direction from where they came. They were in about ten feet of water and could barely see the tops of some of the submerged stumps as the water slopped over them.

"It must be right around here where we hit."

"Whatever you say, Charles. Tell me. You planning to jump in to find it?"

"No. But tell you what we can do. If you use the oars to

keep us right around this spot, I think I can snag that motor."

"Well, that's the damnest thing I've heard of yet!"

"No, listen, KJ," said Charlie. "I've got that big Dardevle with the big treble hooks, and I can rig that up with some of those heavy split shots. Then I'll be able to snag that motor 'cause the water's not very deep here."

KJ reluctantly went along with Charlie's plan and proceeded to keep the boat in the proximity where they had hit. Charlie lowered and raised that weighted-down Dardevle—up and down, back and forth. He literally was jigging for a fifteen horse Evinrude motor. How he got KJ to go along with this scheme nobody ever knew. It may have been because there was nobody else on the water at this time. The two of them, without saying a word to each other, kept at this exercise for close to an hour. Just as unconsciously as they had hit the stump, Charlie suddenly seemed to have come across the motor. He could not easily raise the Dardevle but from looking at the bend of his rod, he had snagged it good. He jerked the rod a couple of times to see how solid it was hooked to the motor, then started to heave heavily. As soon as he did that something solid became alive and quickly took command of the situation with complete authority. It was when their boat was being pulled from where KJ had positioned it that Charlie yelled out.

"Heh, KJ. We're in luck. I think I finally found it."

KJ, ever so stoically and as dryly as the martinis he mixes, said, "Well, if you do, the son-of-a-bitch is still running."

Well, Charlie failed again to land his twenty-pound northern but had far more explaining to do with Brockie about how he lost that motor. KJ interceded as well as he could and told Brockie that Knobby was going to post a sign in the Lounge offering a reward to anyone hooking a 15 horse Evinrude motor in the vicinity of Popple Bay. That didn't sit too well with Brockie either.

So it was with the Happy Hour Bunch. And on their way back home after this trip, and many miles from Knobby's, a voice from the back seat of the car said ever so gently, "We must remember that the oasis of comfort has gotta show up one of these days."

6 The Three Joes

No fishing camp would be complete without someone there being called "Joe." Knobby's camp had three of them. Typically, there was Big Joe and Little Joe. The third member of the group was called Plumb Joe. Actually, Plumb Joe could have been called Mid Joe but that never sounded right so nobody ever called him that, and besides he was a part-time plumber so the nickname came naturally.

As fate would have it the three Joes managed to be in camp at the same time and usually during the holidays. They fished together, always out of an awkward looking barge-like boat that Knobby kept beached at the far side of his landing. Fishing together was the practice until the time Little Joe refused to be in the same boat with the other two. He would go out and fish when they would but always by himself in a separate boat.

This all happened because of the way Big Joe fished. He cast all the time. If they anchored in one place, he would cast. Trolling, drifting, Big Joe still cast which was okay, but it was the way he cast that finally caused Little Joe to depart company. You see, Big Joe could not sit for long due to an irritating and prolonged case of hemorrhoids that had a direct bearing on his disposition. One day Mac McFarland tossed him an inner tube in a gesture of understanding and benevolence. "I don't need that damn thing! Ya think I'm gonna drown?" Big Joe grunted.

"Well, be a pain in the ass. See if I care," Mac retorted.

So to ease his affliction Big Joe stood up when he fished and always positioned himself in the front of the boat. Then he would apply his casting routine. You can't appreciate the words describing his technique, but if you could have seen him in action you would know why Little Joe finally jumped ship. Big Joe cast with a side-arm motion—not overhead but sideways which constantly had the other Joes on guard. Every time he cast the boat would pitch and you could hear a *whissh* as the line whipped over their heads.

Their reaction was automatic, ducking in unison, then awaiting the second phase of Big Joe's technique. Once his lure hit the water, he went into his fast jerk-retrieve-jerk routine. Regardless of the type of lure he used, it skipped across the water as he brought it back toward the boat. More than often it would hit the side of the boat with a sharp clink. The other Joes became battle weary and tried repeatedly to convince him to slow the retrieve.

"Give it a chance to settle, you big lummox," Little Joe demanded.

"He's right. You're making us nervous wrecks," chimed in Plumb Joe.

This urging was of little avail and Big Joe continued to whip the rod sideways and jerk the lure back. They were getting shell shocked until the day Plumb Joe came out wearing a hard hat and gave one to Little Joe. "You guys are real funny. I've never brained you yet," Big Joe said.

"You've come mighty close, you big lummox. Look at the marks on the side of the boat," Little Joe refuted.

"We hope you get the message, Joe," said Plumb Joe.

"Okay, today I'll honestly try doing it your way," said Big Joe.

The other two were not especially optimistic about his promise but sure enough all morning long Big Joe cast more vertically and did let the lure settle. He still jerked it in but not as fast and hard.

What caused Little Joe's departure occurred when Big Joe let his lure settle more than usual and when he retrieved he hooked tightly onto something.

"By God, boys. Maybe your suggestion works. I've got one on," he yelled.

Big Joe put all of his 275 pounds behind his rod and rapidly reeled. His twenty pound test line strained but held fast as he continued reeling in. "He's coming," he yelled. And the others prepared to help land the unseen monster.

"Get ready, boys. He's near the boat," he hollered.

Little Joe was on the net and leaned a little over the side to see if he could tell what Big Joe had on. He dipped the net in the water and said, "Well, bring him up if he's ready."

Big Joe brought up what was on the end of his line with a vicious pull and almost fell out of the boat as the monster shot out of the water fast and solid. It smacked Little Joe right on his hard hat. The impact resounded across the water and knocked Little Joe senseless. Plumb Joe grabbed the line before Big Joe could do anymore damage, then unhooked an 11 × 17 inch waterlogged wooden sign with the words on it, "If the fish isn't big enough to take home whole, then take back a tale."

"Well, whattya know. It's one of your display signs, Big Joe," said Plumb Joe.

"How da hell dat get out here?" he replied.

From then on Little Joe refused to fish with them in their boat and made sure others in camp knew about Big Joe zonking him.

Big Joe Runyon was quite an accomplished sign painter with a thriving business in a town at the southern part of the state. You could tell from his bulk he loved his beer and probably had stock in a brewery. When he painted signs he consumed enough beer to float. You would think this consumption would make his stroke shaky. To the contrary, the more beer he drank the steadier his nerves.

Just as Sam the Chumming Man provided most of the fish mounts in Knobby's Lounge, Big Joe provided most of the signs. His size beguiled the artful delicacy of his signs. He handled a brush with deft, and each sign was a masterpiece of colors, styles, and personalized flourish. For newcomers the Lounge was not only a Piscatorial Museum but also an art exhibit where they could spend considerable time reviewing his signs. "Fisherman's luck—a wet ass and a hungry gut" was not just a bunch of well-lettered words but Big Joe even added an illustrative touch of graphics. "Birds of a feather drink together," "Everyone Here Brings Happiness—some by coming in, others by leaving," "Your best antiques are old friends," and Big Joe's favorite, "Everybody has to believe in something. I believe I'll have another beer."

The three Joes invariably managed to get together at Knobby's during Memorial Day, the Fourth of July, and Labor Day. And true to form you could be certain that signs would begin showing up throughout the entire area some days following their fishing visit. Big Joe painted them and the other Joes handled the distribution. Knobby had to quickly remove the sign he found in one of the cabins that read, "Fish are like company. After three days they stink." He knew damn well that was what caused a group to leave a few days earlier than scheduled.

The Department of Natural Resources and the U.S. Forestry folks also could tell when the three Joes were in

camp. They would find street signs nailed to trees deep in the woods. "State and Madison," "Park Avenue," "Fisherman's Wharf." One sign was found stuck in a sand bar that read, "If you lived here, you'd be home now."

One of the most authentic looking signs was found at the county road just before the two-mile stretch leading to Knobby's. It said, "Until Further Notice Fisherman Are Advised Not To Fish Here." Knobby went into orbit over that one.

And the DNR went into orbit over the official-looking sign that was posted on the old maple tree that guarded the mouth of Stillman's River. It read: "NO FISHING By Order Of WPA (Walleye Protection Agency)." This was one of Big Joe's favorite spots and the definition of WPA was lettered in extra small print.

So maybe some degree of justice prevailed after all when one of Big Joe's signs cracked Little Joe on the noggin. Only thing wrong about the incident was that the wrong Joe got decked.

Little Joe Rosselli lived in these parts all his life. Some of the old timers still remember his football days when he was a star halfback for the high school team that went undefeated for three consecutive years. The state media people never gave the team or Joe much attention since they claimed the small high school never played tough enough competition.

Little Joe would have nothing to do with college. Instead he married the only girl he ever dated and they had two daughters. He worked as a mechanic in a local garage until some business-looking guy got off the train and asked where he could find Joe Rosselli. This guy was putting a football team together to play in a semi-pro barnstorming league throughout the Midwest, and knew about Joe's scat-back ability from a few years ago.

Of course, Joe accepted the offer in spite of his family's opposition, but he left as he said, temporarily, and played football for five months. The squatty runt had piston legs that powered his tough body over the opposition instead of past them. He also excelled as a punter, especially the quick kick and could boot the pigskin as high as an eternity pining the opposing team deep down in their own territory.

The story people who remember Joe tell about him kicking a football to pieces was really no fabrication. It actually happened on a Sunday afternoon in November when the weather was colder than a well digger's ass. Joe's team was leading by two points late in the fourth quarter but were now deep in there own territory on the eight yard line. It was fourth down and Joe went into the normal punt formation standing in his end zone. The snap came fast and Joe, to everyone's surprise, took off running to his right. The opposition was drawn to him. Someone yelled "Kick the shit out of it!" And just before he got to the line of scrimmage, he did exactly that. The ball exploded.

This, quite naturally, brought about considerable confusion. Finally, the officials ruled that the down was to be played over. Again Joe went into punt formation. The snap came and again Joe took off running to his right. The opposing team was not going to be drawn into his ruse again so the line held their ground and the other members dropped back to protect the receiver in order to make the return. But Joe didn't punt this time. He just continued running on and on for eighty yards. From there Joe's team literally sat on the ball and walked off with the win.

Joe left football after that one year stint and went to work in one of the mines and finally for the railroad. He bought a small farm near Knobby's where he could hunt and fish and eventually retire.

His getting konked on the head with one of Big Joe's signs brought to mind another story about Little Joe that Knobby tells quite discreetly and only in the right company. Little Joe enjoyed hunting deer but didn't necessarily follow accepted standards and regulations. One evening he hitched up his horse and wagon and headed off from his farm on one of the old logging roads. Deep in the woods he stopped, tethered his horse to a tree, took his gun and miner's cap, and stepped quietly into the woods to wait for a deer to come down the trail. Many minutes later he heard some slight movement among the trees. He moved toward that direction and turned on the lamp of his miner's cap. The beam picked up a pair of eyes. Little Joe got off a shot, then heard a response of whinnies and a crashing through the woods. "My God!" he thought. "I've shot my horse."

Sure enough his shots splintered branches of a tree next to the horse and it took off tearing through the woods, wagon and all. Joe followed the remains of the wagon back to the barn. It was a long time before that horse trusted him again. From then on Joe concentrated mostly on fishing and hunted only occasionally and only in legal ways.

The third Joe was Joseph Kennedy Dunn whose family was among the original homesteaders in this area. Joe was an only child and was left with several rental properties that sustained his needs more than adequately. He also inherited what was once a successful plumbing business. Not blessed with mechanical ability Joe only dabbled in the plumbing business since as a plumber about the only thing he could do was unclog drains.

Joe Dunn had two aspirations in life. One was to be recognized as an expert fisherman. And the other was to be an accomplished musician. He fell short on both of these goals.

His visits to Knobby's developed an unusual but lasting association with Big and Little Joe, although he and Little Joe had casually known each other for some years having grown up in this area. During one of their fishing outings, he commissioned Big Joe to paint a sign on the door of his old pick-up truck. "You use your own judgement, Joe. I just want to advertise that I'm in the plumbing business," was about all the direction he gave. And he should have known better because those instructions were enough to perk Big Joe's creative juices. The result was an eye-catching slogan complete with appropriate graphics that would turn many an eye on Madison Avenue.

Painted in powder blue and outlined in pink with script subtleties on both doors of the pick-up was: "Plumb Joe Dunn. I'm not really the plumber. I'm the plumber's son. But I can stop the leak until the plumber comes."

Nobody could attest to the amount of business that artwork generated but it certainly got its share of attention. Big Joe thought it was among his best creations and cost Plumb Joe only a case of beer. "I want doss doors when you die or when you get rid of dat pick-up," Big Joe proclaimed. "Dey'll be collectors items some day," he said.

To help satisfy his craving to be a musician Plumb Joe quite often provided entertainment for the entire camp. This happened especially during the holidays. These were times when he organized make-shift bands with anyone in camp who felt inclined to join in. Plumb Joe used spoons, washboards, cow bells, pots and pans, sticks, bottles, horns, brooms, whistles, whatever was available. He was the impresario, giving some semblance of direction and timing, then the band would start playing and it was the most God-awful noise reaching far into the night. No wonder there were less and less bears in this area.

When it wasn't a band Plumb Joe was organizing, it was a sing-a-long. He'd sit in one of the boats with a handcrank phonograph playing one record after another. And all of the camp's whiskey-throated baritones would belt out songs in their best barroom harmony. One of the guys told Plumb Joe one time that he was going to pull some strings and arrange for an audition on the Major Bowes Amateur Hour. Unfortunately, Plumb Joe believed him but fortunately it never happened.

Probably his classic was on a Fourth of July one year when all those in camp were invited to assemble along the boat dock area early in the afternoon to witness an original production called, "The Festival of the Fourth." Big Joe made up several hand-lettered pamphlets advertising the festivities and many families from around the entire area showed up. Even before the program began they were having a good time drinking beer, swapping stories, and having a chance to renew acquaintances.

The opening ceremonies, believe it or not, kicked off with a blast from an old muzzle-loader black powder gun. That quieted things down in a hurry, and as the smoke floated out from the nearby woods, you could see Ralph LeBlanc sneaking around the trees with that old gun. Well, then the beating *rat-a-tat-tat, rat-a-tat-tat* of a drum and the shrill sound of a fife added to the echoing gun blast. What really got the group's attention was the blaring of a bugle blowing out something along the lines of "You gotta get up. You gotta get up . . . You gotta get up in the morning."

This is when the threesome came out of the woods. Little Joe beating on the tom-tom, and dressed in a tattered pair of pants, shirtless with his hairy chest smeared with some of Big Joe's red paint, and wearing a bandanna wrapped around his head. In the middle was Big Joe carrying the American Flag with the pole pushed into his belly. His dress was the same as Little Joe's except he was unpainted. The virtuoso of this trio was the frustrated musician, Plumb Joe, who would toot on the fife for a few notes then blast out on the bugle. It was a performance worthy of Carnegie Hall.

Down the road they marched, past the "Reviewing Stand" consisting of Knobby, Jailer John, and Marge McFarland. They strutted past the people standing along the shore line, across the camping area, and on into the woods on the other side. You would have laughed yourself double seeing this show. The crowd gave them a well-deserved applause, hoot-and-holler, and continued shouts of "More. More. More." You would not have heard it above all the noise from the crowd, but in the woods Big Joe said, "Dat's enough of dat shit." All of this was cut short when Ralph blasted another shot out of the muzzler loader.

The production was the talk of the area and the whole county for years. Plumb Joe could feel proud of himself for the way he pulled it off. The crowd stayed late into the night, drinking lots of beer, laughing, and joking about The Festival of the Fourth. Knobby grilled venison and bratswurst and roasted potatoes. Some firecrackers got shot off and the muzzle loader popped once or twice until the last blast knocked Ralph off his feet. Then things quieted down and people returned to their homes or to their cabins. Laid out in Knobby's Lounge were the three Spirits of '76 snoozing and snoring their way through the night. Ironically, over their heads was one of Big Joe's signs. It read: "There's No Fool Like A Fishing Fool."

7 | Marge, Sit Down. You're Rocking The Boat

It took many years until a few of the heartier women skewed up enough courage to venture into Knobby's Camp, and it was more like their husbands who had the courage to bring them in the first place. Records are not available to document who the first woman was to come to Knobby's on a fishing trip since it was known that a few of the native women dropped in from time to time, but in recent years more and more have been showing up with their husbands. Although it was never advertised as such, Knobby's was always an equal opportunity fishing camp, and Knobby along with some of the more hardened others will admit that their presence hasn't been all too bad. Besides, most of them could outfish the men anyway as was the situation with Mac and Marge McFarland.

Outwardly, anyone hearing Mac, and you couldn't help

but hear him, would think they were completely incompatible. It was Mac who unrelentlessly seemed to have it in for Marge all the time. "For Crisake, Marge, Sit down!" he would bark out in a way that carried his voice all over the lake. Marge would softly reply, "But, Mac, I haven't stood up yet."

If it wasn't "Sit down," it would be "Keep still" or "Why didn't you go before we got out here?" In each and every instance a "For Crisake, Marge" would punctuate Mac's verbal harassment.

But in spite of the seemingly hostility Mac displayed, they were very close to one another. Married for almost forty years. Grandparents. Church members. Respected residents of a medium size rural community. It must have been the tranquility of Knobby's environment that brought out Mac's yelling at Marge. He never did it at home. He knew he couldn't get by with it. Most newcomers to the camp would at first be embarrassed at the treatment Marge seemed to get from her husband, some to the point of almost wanting to say something to Mac. However, after you got to know the McFarlands you could see through his crust and realized the "bark was far worse than the bite."

If the truth were known, the reason Mac barked like he did was because Marge always caught more fish than he did. She never would admit to this and accepted Mac's vocalizing as his way to let everyone know that supposedly he still wore the pants in this family.

His full and official name was Homer Amos McFarland but only Marge and members of the immediate family were aware of this moniker. Everything he did requiring a signature, address, whatever, was always "H. A. McFarland." And many a time someone would say without his hearing, "That old HAM is at it again." Even Marge almost forgot his full name, and only when pushed to the ultimate breaking point would she ever call him "Homer Amos." When she did, it was guaranteed to get attention.

Mac was tall and lean with a cranky lined face topped by a crew-cut that had become white since his sergeant days in World War II. He was known in the accounting business as a "bean counter" having worked for thirty years as a clerk, accountant, and finally as corporate treasurer of this small company that made heaters, fans, and ventilator products. He retired when his firm was bought out, and at his recognition dinner Mac was given the thing he cherished most and had been closest to for all those years with the firm—his oak captain-type desk chair. And the first thing he did was to have that chair mounted to the rear seat of his fishing boat. People seeing Mac's boat tied up to the dock with the oak chair overlooking everything would shake their heads in amazement, and maybe with some envy since it was comfortable.

Marge was the absolute Mother, Housewife, Friend, Volunteer. Completely opposite her husband. She was involved, outgoing, generally interested in everything. It was Marge that got Mac interested in fishing even before he retired. Her brother and his wife found Knobby's Place one summer while driving on one of the half-hidden county roads through the woods. They fell in love with the peace and quiet, the serene remoteness, and of course, the fishing. Marge felt Mac needed to reduce his business diet, take some vacation, so she arranged for them to spend a week with her brother and wife the following summer. That was not a particularly good idea since Mac and his brother-in-law had differing opinions on every subject, at least Mac had the contrary opinions. They even argued one whole day and on into the night whether scaling a fish was better than filleting. Mac knew little if nothing about the subject but the more 90 proof he poured down the more he became the noted authority.

That all led into the next morning when Mac, Marge, and the brother-in-law went out fishing together. Mac sat in his desk chair and continued preaching from that special pulpit. Marge sat in the middle, and the brother-in-law in the front. Each of them had two poles, assorted tackle, and minnows and worms along with a fresh bottle of 90 proof. They anchored at the edge of a weed bed where Mac claimed he had caught a lot of fish.

"I'm gonna use red worms," said the brother-in-law.

"Hell, not me. Marge, hand me the minnow bucket," barked Mac. Marge rigged up with nightcrawlers and like the men had a pole out on both sides of the boat. She was kept busy passing things back and forth—the minnow bucket, red worms, and the 90 proof. The men paid her little attention. She was along for the ride and to cater to their needs.

"Got anything yet?" yelled Mac.

"You'll know when I do," replied the brother-in-law.

After some time in this spot Mac was ready to move on but then Marge got a bite and pulled in a jumbo perch. Mac said, "Well, let's get the hell out of this place. They're not biting." Then on the other pole Marge got a nice walleye. Another perch. Another walleye.

"For Crisake, Marge. Do you think you can stop long enough to pass me that bottle?" Mac sputtered.

The interruption didn't stall Marge. Up she pulled a perch, then a walleye, perch, walleye. After twenty minutes of this pole-to-pole action Marge caught several perch and walleyes. Mac said it was definitely time to leave since the only activity he and the brother-in-law had was lowering the level in the 90 proof bottle.

Nearing the shore by their cabin, the brother-in-law jumped out unsteadily onto shore and proceeded to pull the boat in. He then walked down the dock to where Mac was about to step out, but before he could tie up the rear of the boat Mac was astraddle doing the splits. One foot on the dock and one foot still in the boat which was slowly and agonizingly moving farther from the dock.

"Hey, give me a hand before my crotch gives!" Mac yelled.

The brother-in-law broke out laughing. "Maybe you'd better give Mac a hand," Marge said. "I'd hate to see that happen."

Well, you could have predicted what would happen next. The brother-in-law finally grabbed Mac's hand and tried to pull him up on the dock. Mac came out of the boat but his weight was now distributed in such a way that he forced the brother-in-law from the dock and both of them landed in the water.

"For Crisake, Marge," Mac grunted as the two of them stood up in the water and waded to shore. Mac turned and said to Marge, "And be sure you don't fillet those fish."

That was the last time the four of them shared a cabin and fished out of the same boat although they still managed to spend a lot of time together at Knobby's. Mac and Marge bought a small house trailer and parked it in the woods in the camping area. Mac and the brother-in-law continued arguing in later years but on fewer and fewer subjects.

The only other special and personal item the McFarland's added to their boat besides that oak desk chair of Mac's was a small porcelain pot or "pee can" as Mac called it. This was Marge's commode that Mac had actually purchased for her as a Christmas present since she was having him pull in to shore too often. The commode was tucked down in the front of the boat behind the seat very conveniently for Marge. This little gesture on Mac's part extended his fishing time and softened his disposition. Actually, he was quite pleased with the way his purchase worked out and he delighted in yelling across the lake, "Marge is peeing now!" Of course, nobody would ever know this since Marge was quite inconspicuous in her position and she just kept on doing her job without a thought of adding more to what Mac was trying to make of it.

One cool September day Mac did get the best of her. A couple of cups of coffee for breakfast, more from the thermo in their boat, the cold wind, and Marge moved to the front of the boat for her toilet. The only other boat on the water was several hundred yards away and with Marge's experience and dexterity with her derriere they never would suspect what she was doing. And Mac was less frequently inclined to tell the world what she was doing. Marge nestled down on that porcelain pot, much relieved.

It was then Mac got a strike on one of his poles. At least he pretended to have a strike since the way he fished you could never really tell. He leaned from his chair for the pole. "That's gotta be a bass," he yelled loud enough for the other boat on the lake to take notice. Mac pulled hard to set the hook but typically he missed the strike.

"For Crisake, Marge. Look what you made me do."

All this commotion in the boat forced Marge more securely on the commode which was now firmly wedged under the front seat. She looked up at Mac, her legs awkwardly draped over the seat. "Mac, I can't get up."

"Well, what did you do now, Marge?"

"I'm stuck."

"Well, stay where you are. Maybe I can help."

"Mac, I ain't going anyplace. Just help me up."

Instead of getting up to help Marge, he went and started the motor, gunned it, and headed out to the middle of the lake toward the other boat.

"Where you going? I need help, Mac."

"That's where I'm going to get you help. Those two guys in that boat can help us get you off that thing."

Marge turned slightly and saw Mac heading straight for the other boat. "Stop this now!" she screamed. Mac heard her all right but kept on going almost 100 yards away from the

two fishermen. Marge was getting more and more concerned and took a deep breath, reached and grabbed the seat and started to pull forward with all her strength. That was exactly when Mac cut the motor. Off the commode popped Marge to a position where she was doing a beautiful job of mooning the two fishermen. Mac made a wide swing so they could get a full view then he headed in. He tried to contain himself as long as he could but finally cut loose laughing so hard he couldn't keep the boat straight. You can imagine how much he made of that incident with the rest of the bunch at Knobby's. "You shoulda seen Marge mooning those two," he kept repeating.

This was typical of the kind of escapades Mac and Marge had everytime they were at Knobby's. During the years, Mac mellowed much and Marge tried to be even more helpful to him in spite of his pleadings against her assistance.

One year it had been unseasonably dry and by mid-September fishing parties had to cope with several sandbars that were becoming apparent in the shallower water. Mac and Marge had gone out in mid-morning one pleasant day and planned to have lunch on shore. She had taken a thermos of soup and some sandwiches and a bottle of wine. They fixed a fire on shore, lazily lounged on the sand beach, and took in the foliage that was beginning to turn orange, red, yellow. It was late in the afternoon when they headed in and Mac was acting like a rejuvenated teenager. He had the motor going at top speed and moved the boat crisply over the water. He zigged and zagged the boat and rounded the last of three small islands. It was then that everything catapulted to the front of the boat as the entire unit crunched to an abrupt stop in the sand.

"For Crisake, Marge. What did you do now?"

Marge raised herself from the bottom of the boat and could see Mac holding onto the desk chair. "Looks like we hit a sandbar," she said. Mac roared back, "Well, who the hell put it there?"

They raised the motor, and rocked and rocked the boat hoping to work enough water underneath it to make it more buoyant. Both of them took the oars and pushed in cadence against the sand. Neither of these exercises did much good and they were still aground. Mac decided to get out into the water and tried to push the rear of the boat free. He was getting nowhere and finally realized Marge had moved to the rear where Mac was struggling. "Mac, is there something I can do, dear?"

"Hell, yeah. Get in the front of the boat and push with that oar against the sand."

Gradually the boat eased into slightly deeper water even

though Marge still had a death grip on that oar. "Mac, I can't get the oar out of the sand," she said straining to pull the oar free. Mac climbed over the seats and literally over Marge. "Here give me that damn oar."

Mac pulled hard on the oar the same time Marge released her grip. The oar shot out of the sandbar with Mac still holding the shaft. It was on a direct course toward Marge and hit her square in the mouth. For once Mac said nothing.

Marge looked up at him through watery eyes, and with bloodied lips said controllably, "Homer Amos McFarland. Without a doubt. Beyond any question whatsoever. You are the most dangerous man I have ever met . . . yet I don't know what I would to without you. Now, for Crisake, Mac. Can we go in so I can take care of this?"

8 | The Italian Connection

Every one of the personalities at Knobby's Camp had their little peculiarities, but undoubtedly one of the most mysterious of the groups that regularly fished here was a party of four appropriately referred to as "The Italian Connection." A first glance at this foursome and you would think they were ancestors of the original Sons of Italy. Nobody openly talked about it but the overwhelming opinion was that these guys had connections with the Mafia. You could tell by their habits they were straddling the shady side. On the other hand, maybe this was all pure imagination so there would be something to talk about like telling the family you fished with members of the Mafiosa.

It was only after several years that their specific names became more and more pronounceable, but they would always be referred to by the clever nicknames the guys at Knobby's had tagged them with. Nobody tried very hard to pronounce every syllable in their surnames. It just flowed out as best it could. They never signed Knobby's register like most others, and always got their fishing licenses somewhere else if they had any at all. Of course, nobody dared to question them about this very minor detail.

Tony "Tough Nut" Tufano, outwardly seemed to be the take-charge guy. Always emotionally in command of the situation. Although small and slight, Tony gave the orders, and, as authority would have it, usually caught the most fish of the group. The word around camp was that Tony's grandfather used Knobby's camp many years ago to get away on various occasions from certain business predicaments. It was also said that the senior Tufano put up the money to help Knobby keep the place going when he was first starting up. This was something nobody ever talked to Knobby about because where he got the money was really no concern to any of the regular guys coming here. If Tufano wanted a hideaway, this place was ideal. And if young Tony wanted to follow the same path that was okay also.

Then there was Vito "The Nose" Giovannetti. It was obvious why he was called this. His nose was the dominating part of his entire body. Although Vito was overall large and fleshy, putting over two hundred pounds on his five foot five frame, it was his nose that got most of the attention. It was just plain big and bulbous. Apparently, Vito was very well off financially and had the right kind of ancestral connections that attached him to the others in this group. His dollar attributes outweighted his other traits. He was the loudest, funniest, and the butt of the group's jokes. However, the verbal abuse would go just so far since they were all well aware of Vito's influence at home.

The other two members of the group seemed to go along for the ride and were the tote-and carry types. Go for this, go for that. Start the fire, run the motor, cook the food, wash the dishes. Vinnie "Santy" Santucci took care of the domestic chores around their cabin. And Carmine "The Caddy" Calabrese did the mechanical duties like driving the car, running the boat. Carmie was the only one who ventured out of the cabin for any length of time during the day. This was primarily to brush off the pine needles from the car, give it a wipe here and there, chat with Sam the Chummer, and to check out the boat.

The Italian Connection spent about ten days in camp about three times during summer. More if business situations demanded it. They hated cold weather. For them it was July, August, and sometimes early September. You never knew exactly when this would be but Knobby always had their place reserved and ready to move in. They invariably arrived late at night or very early in the morning. The next day you would see a sleek, immaculately clean, black Cadillac parked outside their cabin and tucked away under the evergreens. How they could drive down Knobby's road without getting their tires dirty was another of their mysteries.

Tony, Vito, Vinnie, and Carmie. They always stayed at "Breezy Point," a plain vanilla-type cabin with beds for four, inside john, a kitchen and eating room combined. The reason it was called "Breezy Point" was because it was situated on the stretch of ground that jutted out farthest into the lake. It was bordered by water on three sides, and some seventy-five yards from the next cabin. It was also the first cabin Knobby had constructed in camp for "Joie Tough" Tufano.

You never heard them unload. You just knew they had arrived. The shades were always pulled down, and how Knobby managed all those years to rig up two floodlights at opposite ends of the cabin without anyone knowing about it, is another of the mysteries. It was said that when this group fished at night these floodlights were to help them find their way back to Breezy Point. At least, that is what Knobby said but why didn't the other cabins have lights? When these guys left, down would come the floodlights. We often wondered why he didn't keep them up permanently but he always got that job done by himself and nobody ever asked him. Guess it was a perk that came with their reservation.

Most of the camp never bothered these guys for good reason. Being on the wrong side of the law was one thing but being on the wrong side of the Mafisoa was another, and besides they didn't seem to want to socialize. One particular incident made it clear they wanted to be left alone. It was one of the many nights when the Happy Hour Bunch had consumed enough courage to see what would happen if the Italian Connection were forced into action. Two of the Happy Hour guys took one of the boats and rowed out into the lake just far enough to be away from full exposure to the floodlights. The two of them in the boat had rigged up a catapult kind of contraption, and lofted a handful of small stones onto the roof of Breezy Point. When those stones hit and rolled down the roof, all hell must have broken loose inside. You would have thought Mount Etna had erupted. Out the front door bolted Vinnie and Carmie, heading for the Cadillac. They were not carrying six and a half foot Garcia spinning rods, but more like cut-down double barreled, twelve guage Berettas. Tony yelled out instruction in Italian. Off went the lights in Breezy Point. You could see a window raise very slowly and then Vito peered out, at least his nose did.

It wasn't until early in the morning did the camp settle down. The Happy Hour Bunch slept heavily and confidently through all the commotion. When daylight came the next day Breezy Point was vacated. The Cadillac was gone and so were the floodlights. Knobby didn't say anything to the Happy Hour Bunch but he sure had his suspicions as to what may have happened.

Say what you will about the quirks of Tony, Vito, Vinnie, and Carmie. Most of the time they came to Knobby's to really fish and worked hard at it when they did which was usually at night. Anyone of the regulars will tell you that live bait worked best on the lake. Minnows, chubs, worms, leeches, nightcrawlers. But you couldn't convince these guys. Plugs, poppers, spoons, spinners were their forte. And, you know, they did pretty well with the artificals on largemouths and northerns.

It was during the first week in August when the Italian Connection showed their true colors. The weather had been unbearbly hot and muggy, and the fish just stopped doing anything. Even the kids on the dock couldn't hook a perch or bluegill. Knobby's turned into a swimming hole instead of a fishing camp. Guys would wade in the water along the beach or take a boat out and swim rather than fish.

But Tony, Vito, Vinnie, and Carmie were night fishermen, and the betting was that if anyone were going to catch fish in this weather it would be them. A summer rain had stopped late in the afternoon and about seven o'clock the Italian Connection went out loaded in one boat bound and determined they were going to catch some fish. Four tackle boxes, seven rods—Vito had to have three light, medium, and stiff—two bottles of Chianti, and Carmie running the motor.

The water had calmed and settled once the wind died down, and their plan was to head down to the far end of the lake and work their way back by fishing the shoreline. At least, that's the way Tony had it mapped out. Naturally, a nip or two out of the Chianti jug was also the order of the evening. It was lukewarm dark when they stopped and started casting. According to Tony's plan, he would cast first, then Vinnie, then Vito. One at a time. Never together so their lines wouldn't get all tangled. Carmie strictly ran the motor and positioned the boat. You could imagine all the instructions he was going to get.

After they had drained the second Chianti bottle they got down to some serious casting. Tony missed two that hit short, then Vinnie caught a bass on a Jitterbug near some stumps.

"You luck ass!" yelled Vito.

A few casts later Tony missed another strike right after his popper bounced off of some rocks. "Too bad, luck butt," Vito complained. When Vinnie caught his second bass, Vito got pissed off. "We gotta change places. You guys are always in the front and I'm back here with this goof ball. You better start putting me on some fish, Carm-ass, or you'll walk home."

"They're not in open water, Vito. Fish the shore more."

"Shut your mouth and drive the boat."

"You're not getting it close enough to shore," snapped Tony. To which Vito roughly replied, "Yeah, but I don't want to get all hung up with this goof ball driving the boat."

"Can you make out those rocks where the tree drops down into the water?" asked Tony. "Toss it over there close."

"Throw toward the tree," barked Vinnie.

"Shit! I can't hardly see that tree."

"Well, throw it out and count to three before you brake."

"You shut up your face and drive the boat."

Vito cast and reeled in. He cast again, and again, and again. "Now what the hell wrong am I doing?"

"You expect a hit on every cast for one thing."

"You're still out too far. They should be feeding right against the shore. We're coming to a choice spot now near those small willows, Vito. None of us will fish. You toss it right at the base of those willows. They've got to be feeding around there."

"And get it closer this time," Carmie said. Well, Vito got it close on his next cast all right. His Flatfish smacked deep into the willows and he was hung up tight.

"Somma bitch! See what happened when I get it close?"

It would be an understatement to say he was angry. Vito stiffened, pulled hard, and although the line gave with the bending of the willow branch, he couldn't free the Flatfish.

"Jiggle your rod."

"I don't need anymore of your advice."

"Slack off and jerk it hard."

"You go jerk it off," yelled Vito who was now good and mad. He decided to put his over two hundred pounds behind pulling that ten pound test line as hard as he could away from the willow. He leveled the rod straight out, cranked the reel pulling back on the rod at the same time. The line was now stretched tighter than a bull's ass in fly time.

BOOOWAAANG . . . . .

Out of that willow branch like an arrow shot the Flatfish, heading directly toward Vito and his humongous nose. Vito never saw a thing. Like the sound of a rotten apple hitting the pavement, both sets of trebles imbedded themselves in the fatest part of his nose. Only Carmie's strong arm kept Vito from pitching out of the boat.

"Somma bitch! Look what you bastards did to me now."

Tony, Vinnie, and Carmie couldn't restrain themselves and unaminously burst out with a laugh that sent ripples out into the water. Carmie squeezed his knees tightly together to hold back his gut-wrenching delight.

"Holy Mother of God! I'm bleeding. Get this boat outta here." Carmie put the seven and a half horse motor into high gear and headed toward Breezy Point. The roar of the motor muffled their laughter.

"Get me to a doctor fast. I think lockjaw's setting in."

Tony was almost jetted from the front of the boat as it hit the beach full speed in front of their cabin. Most people didn't know what all the fussing was about at Breezy Point but could sure tell something was bothering the Italian Connection.

Tony cut the line and left Vito standing there by the Cadillac with the Flatfish hanging from his nose. Then Tony, Vinnie, and Carmie packed up their belongings in the greatest of hurry and off they went. They stopped only long enough to ask Knobby directions to the nearest doctor. That's when Knobby saw the Flatfish impaled in Vito's nose. Oh, did he try to keep a straight face.

Everything turned out okay. Vito didn't get lockjaw and the whole thing was really a blessing in disguise. When the Italian Conneciton returned to camp in July that next year, Vito seemed to be a new man. At least he looked like a new man what with one of the best looking nose jobs you could imagine . . . considerably flatter.

9 The Flatulentors

Willis Philpott, Herm Eschner, and Kazzy Kazimier always made it for opening day of fishing season. At least, for the last fifteen years or so they spent that week here fishing and doing what they did so well when away from home ... exercising their anal orifices or what's known as farting. If awards were ever handed out for this intestinal phenomena, the three of them probably would hold world records or at a minimum, undoubtedly Guinness records for the loudest, longest, and most frequent farts.

They came the farthest away to fish Knobby's taking a day and a half to make the trip. Nobody ever got near their car when it first arrived since you could imagine the odor that must have prevailed inside.

Each year they occupied the cabin called Northern Air which was appropriate for their passing gas peculiarities but it was never really planned that way. It was one of those oddities that worked out. After all, they could have been assigned to Breezy Point but it was always booked. Northern Air was close to the cabin that was occupied on opening day by Ralph LeBlanc and his motly group of Jailer John, Doctor DuCette,

Fibber Farquahar, Tonto Tom, and Little Joe, and when both of those groups got together it was something that kept you in perpetual belly warming stitches.

Nobody at Knobby's would ever deny that Willis, Herm, and Kazzy were not diehard fishermen and their stringers always attested to that. They were up before the crack of dawn and out in their boat before most of the other fishermen were stirring. And they stayed out all day getting in as much fishing as they could regardless of the kind of weather. Those staying in cabins near the waters edge would make it a point to be up and awake in order to hear this threesome take off.

Invariably, just after they loaded their boat Willis would let a boomer of a fart fly. It sounded like an old rotten log had broken in two.

"Okay, who fart?" Kazzy had an aversion to anyone making a noise when farting and was always quick to point a finger at the other two.

"Willis?"

"Not me. You fart, Herm?"

"Who? Me? Fart?"

"Someone farted. You could hear it all over the lake."

"It wasn't me. You fart, Willis?"

"Well, not enough to notice. They do slip out once in awhile."

"Get your butt in the boat," Kazzy commanded, "and let's get some fishing in."

As close as these three were once they started fishing hardly ever a word was said. Not even a "getting any bites?", "maybe we ought to try over there", "doing any good?" They just understood each other that well, and took it for granted that Kazzy, who always ran the boat, would put them on fish. It was only when either Willis or Herm would lean over to pull in the minnow bucket that their solitude would be broken by a sputtering, popping sound. It was a series of farts that stopped once Willis or Herm sat up straight and put on a fresh minnow. The sputtering started up all over again when one or the other put the bucket back in the water.

"I heard you that time, Willis."

"What?"

"You know. You let one of your poppers out."

"Not me. Musta been Herm."

"It wasn't me. I haven't moved."

"Well, maybe I did sneak one out," Willis admitted. "It had to be something we had for breakfast."

"I had the same as you," Kazzy replied. "Why don't I fart like you guys?"

"You don't eat right."

"And it's because you use all those dumb bitters in your Manhattans."

Just then Kazzy's line made a discernible jerk, then another, and another. The line became taut and Kazzy could feel it firmly against the rod tip. He raised the rod carefully until it quivered and the line moved confidently and laterally from the boat.

Herm was sitting next to Kazzy watching the tension. "Set the hook," he said.

Kazzy did just that and the line zinged out crisply then down into the depths of the water. "Hot diggity damn. I've got a good one on," Kazzy shouted.

His fishing rod was gyrating with every darting, dashing movement the fish made. Down deeper the fish went. The drag was absorbing a lot of the pressure and Kazzy patiently played the fish to its limits.

"Better get the net. I think he's ready to come in."

A few more resisting pulls then Kazzy stood up to bring the fish into the net that Herm held. As he did he released one of those semi-silent slider farts that squeak like a door hinge.

"You say something, Kazzy?"

"No. Just get that net ready."

"You hear something, Willis? Like a tennis shoe skidding on a gym floor."

"Yeah. I heard a squeaky squeak. Sounded like a fart moving sideways."

"Herm, pay attention to the net. I'm bringing it in."

Herm dipped the landing net and scooped up a beautiful five pound walleye. Willis and Herm smiled at each other. "Nice wallie, Kaz," said Herm.

"Nice fart," Willis remarked.

Of the three of them there was no question that Willis' farts were always the loudest, most violent, raucous, and un-predictable. Once he let go an ear-splitting boomer so suddenly at the bait shop outside of town that the owner who was upstairs at the time came rushing down excitedly wondering if his gas line had popped. It smelled as if it had. All the water in the minnow tanks rippled momentarily. Willis said something about stubbing his toe on the bottom of one of the tanks. Herm and Kazzy did little to defend the incident. They looked at the owner and pointed to Willis and Herm said, "He's a clumsy old fart."

Knobby certainly could attest to Willis' talent for letting go with pungent, untimely, sonic boomers. A lot of the guys were sitting around in Knobby's Lounge one cool night swapping fish stories. There was a fire going in the fireplace to take out the chillness. Fibber Farquahar was telling a story about how he shot a ten pound largemouth bass as it leaped out of the water after a frog. "But as I jumped in the water to get it, there was this huge alligator looking at me, so I. . . ."

The Fibber never got to finish the story. There was a thunderous *BAARROOOOM!* And in unison the entire fire-place area was vacated. All of them claimed they saw phos-phorescent sparks coming at them. Willis remained standing there sheepishly by himself.

Knobby would tell the summertime crowd that if Willis Philpott were there when the weather was dry and the dust inches thick on his road, his farts were powerful enough to blow off the dust all the way to the county road.

Herm Eschner could not hold a candle to Willis when it came to the decibel level of farts. But you could hear Herm fart, all right, and he pulled no punches in admitting it. The difference between Herm and Willis was in articulation. Herm could fart, then look at the nearest person around and say something that would make them almost apologize or feel embarrassed because Herm let out the breezer in the first place.

One late afternoon when the sun was behind the evergreens Herm took their stringer to the fish shack. It was his turn to do the cleaning. The only person there was old Sam the Chummer bent over the table cleaning his fish. Herm entered the screened-in shack and turned on the dim light.

"Sam, you need some light on the subject."

No acknowledgement from Sam. He just kept cleaning his fish, scaling each one meticulously, then surgically gutting them. He had scales everywhere and fish entrails all over the table. Herm could see sharing the fish shack with Sam would be an arduous, hour or more affair.

"You cut some mustard, Sam?" Herm yelled since he knew Sam couldn't hear worth a toot.

"What the hell you mean?"

"You know, did you cut some cheese? Did you fart? Smells like someone farted in here."

"You're crazy! I'm just cleaning my fish."

Herm knew some skunks had holed up under the shack, and although they never bothered anyone they still posed a nuisance occasionally. There was always a faint odor of their presence around the shack. "Well, if you didn't fart, Sam, one of those skunks must have."

Herm started in cleaning the fish. And after he had a few of them done, he let go with a king-size popperino. Even Willis would have been proud of the tonal quality. It oozed out at an alto level then exploded several octaves lower. Herm waggled his fillet knife in front of Sam. "What did you do, Sam? Belch in your pants."

Sam still had not reacted. He never heard a word but finally he did look up, squinted, and kind of turned up his nose. "I think I'll get the hell out of here. Those skunks are starting to move around."

Herm had another habit the other two could not duplicate as well. He could burp like nobody else. All three of them loved their beer but when Herm tipped the bottle to his mouth it was like a steady mountain stream flowing into a waiting pool below. He never swallowed. When he finished he would smile, punch his stomach, open his mouth wide, and erucate long and loud. He loved to do this because he felt it was more obnoxious than a fart. Farts, he believed, sometimes came unpredictably and he liked to plan when he was going to belch. And it always delighted him to apologize afterwards, "Excuse me, excuse me, from the bottom of my heart. If I hadn't belched it would have been a fart."

The truth of the matter was that Kazzy Kazimier was the most proficient and skillful of the three when it came to passing gas, although he would never admit to that. After three or four Manhattans, a couple of beers, and some of Willis' cooking he could give anyone a run for their money. And that's what he did at the poker game held in their cabin.

For some reason not a lot of poker was played at Knobby's. The regulars just didn't indulge in the game preferring to tell stories, drink their beer, and do funny other things. They felt they could always play poker and only got away from home a few times to unwind and recharge their batteries on these fishing trips.

About the only time a genuine poker game took place was when Ralph LeBlanc's group and this threesome got together. The card players were Doctor DuCette, The Fibber, Tonto Tom, Little Joe, Jailer John, Herm and Kazzy. Ralph and Willis took care of the refills and stood around and watched. This one night in particular Kazzy really shined. After putting away several helpings of Willis' best beans and brastwurst meals he was more than pleasantly filled.

The poker game started around nine o'clock in the Northern Air cabin on this cool evening. It was always nickel-dime poker so nobody ever got severely hurt financially if they behaved themselves. And it was always straight poker—five, six, seven card stud. No wild games. One year the Fibber tried to introduce a game called, "Between The Sheets." It was so complicated they all quit and went to Knobby's Lounge. Then once Tonto Tom tried to explain a game called "Indian" where the players hold up one card on the top of their head and that becomes their wild card only they can't see it so they don't know what it is. That game never worked either and it was Doctor DuCette who took out his fillet knife and pretended he was going to scalp Tonto Tom.

Anyway this particular poker game had been going for about two hours and The Fibber was dealing seven-card stud, first two cards down, four cards up, and the last card down. Little Joe had been having a string of bad luck while the others were about even, with Kazzy the big winner thus far. After the fourth card was dealt all the players had the makings of a winning hand. The Fibber dealt the fifth card and the betting became more exciting. Ralph and Willis wandered around quietly inspecting the player's hands. The Fibber dealt the sixth card.

"Okay. Pot right? Last card up."

"Doc, four of spades. Looks like you got all black there."

(He would need one more spade for his flush).

"A king to you, Tonto. We're looking at maybe two pair." (Tonto had a king and a ten as his hole cards and a ten showing).

"And there's a possible straight, Herm." (He would need a seven on his last down card).

"John, you luck ass. Here's your third nine. You're in the driver's seat now." (That's all he had in the six cards dealt).

"A five spot, Kazzy. Can't make much of that." (Kazzy had a bust kind of hand. Only a pair of queens but that wouldn't win this pot).

"Ace of hearts, Little Joe. Suppose you'll be bumping again." (He had two back-to-back aces as his hole cards and had raised the best on the last three cards dealt).

"And the dealer gets a ten to go with his nine, eight, seven for a possible straight."

"Okay, John. Your bet."

When it got to Little Joe he raised, then Doc raised, around to Little Joe and he raised again.

"This is the best pot of the night, boys. Someone's going to get well on this one. Okay, last card down."

Doc got a diamond stopping his spade flush.

Tonto got the last ten for a full house—three tens and two kings. He was already fingering his bets.

Herm was dealt the seven he needed to complete the eight high straight.

The cards were flowing right and Jailer John got the fourth nine and he hunched closer to the kitchen table ready to bet.

Kazzy got a deuce for an absolutely nothing hand.

Little Joe could hardly contain himself. He peeked at his third hole card and it was the fourth ace.

The Fibber also dealt himself a bust hand.

"Okay, let's see who the players are."

John opened the betting. Kazzy called for no reason probably because he was concentrating on an impending expulsion of flatus. After Little Joe raised the bet Kazzy downed the rest of his beer in one gulp. The Fibber folded. Doctor DuCette called the bet. Tonto raised Little Joe's bet. Kazzy wiggled a little in his chair.

"I'm taking the last raise, boys," hollered Herm. Everyone tossed their betting into the pot. Kazzy raised slightly in his chair putting most of his weight on the left cheek of his ass. You could see four grown men now hunched over the table looking greedily at one another, then to their cards, and the pile of money. Kazzy wasn't exactly hunched over the table. He was more or less leaning to one side. At the precise moment when The Fibber told John to declare Kazzy sneaked out a silent geyser of hot, pent up intestinal gas. It first flowed downward around the card player's ankles, then upwards wrapping its invisible stinking cloud around the table and the players. The veiled vapors permeated their clothing. It smarted their eyes. Its bizarre odor was reminiscent of a paper mill and a meat packing plant processing their products simultaneously. It penetrated their nasal passages and sent stifling sulfur dioxide signals to their brain cells.

"Who died?"

"Holy shit!"

"God almighty! It's an attack."

Willis couldn't budge the windows. Jailer John covered his nose and mouth with his hands. Ralph bolted out the door and barfed. The mist persisted until its suffocating stench overpowered the remaining players.

"A month old cadaver wouldn't smell worse," murmured the Doctor as he left. The Fibber got a coughing spell. Tonto stormed out of the cabin gasping for a breath of fresh air. Little Joe's face was now beet red from holding his breath. He wanted that poker pot but threw his cards in the air and rushed out of the cabin yelling, "Even the bears couldn't stand that stink."

The only one left was Kazzy. "Come on, guys. Let's get on with the game."

A few years after that LeBlanc came over to their Northern Air cabin and announced that his group challenged this threesome to a farting contest, and asked if they would accept the challenge. "You bet your sweet ass we will," replied Willis knowing he could out fart anyone in the area. But when LeBlanc explained that the contest would have more creativity than just letting explosive boomers fly, Willis started to back off.

"Doc suggests we see who is the best at setting a fart on fire. You pick someone and our guys will. We'll have the contest in two nights at your place."

Herm jumped at the opportunity and said, "You're on.

And the prize will be that losers will clean all the fish caught by the winners for a week." LeBlanc agreed knowing the Doctor had something up his sleeve. Kazzy was noncommittal for the time being.

Tonto Tom was one of the contestants and for two days he remained in their cabin. Didn't even go out to wet a line. The Doctor was continually filling him up with a mixture of vegetables—broccoli, cabbage, cauliflower, and bananas and raisins, and quantities of prune juice in the morning. In between he consumed enough beer to support a brewery. All the while the Doctor kept him off the potty.

Kazzy was appointed to perform the honors for the Northern Air cabin and didn't put up much of a fuss. He knew they would win since Willis special concoction called "Hoe Down Chowder" would blow the top off manhole covers. It contained chopped up German sausage, tomatoes, onions, garlic, and just about every variety of beans—Navy, Lima, Kidney, Garbanzo, Barley, Pinto. Willis would also add more than a dash or two of beer as it was cooking.

The night of the fart contest arrived and they all gathered at Northern Air. Doctor DuCette set out the official rules, distributed the official candles told the witnesses to take their seats, and introduced the two combatants—Tonto Tom and Kazzy—each of whom looked ten pounds heavier. The cabin was completely dark and Tonto was taken to the bathroom where he dropped his drawers and got a pep talk by The Doctor. The Doctor led him back out, lit the candle, told Tonto to bend over and on the count of three to let it go. One . . . two . . . three. It was quiet as an unoccupied church, then you could distinguish a definite wheez or the carbonation from soda bottle. And, sure enough, there was a tinge of blue flame as the burning candle ignited the escaping flatus.

It was only a momentary phenomenon. Maybe only two seconds at the most but everyone roared, clapped, and slapped Tonto on his back and buttocks. He then relaxed in a series or burps and farts. "You done good, Tonto," The Doctor proudly said.

Now it was Kazzy's turn to defend the honors of Northern Air. Willis led him into the bathroom where he was prepped. What Willis did was to have Kazzy bend over so he could insert the tip of a small hand pump used to pump up kerosene lamps. A couple of jabs and Kazzy was ready for action.

At first, when the count of three was reached, you could detect a noticeable hissing sound, then a slight sputtering, and then a narrow, luminescent streak much like that of a blow torch. There was never a question about the winner. Kazzy's flame was longer and more lasting. Even Tonto was impressed although he never saw how well he himself had performed.

After that they all got pretty well loaded and gathered at Knobby's Lounge where the Doctor bought all the beers and they told everyone there about their accomplishments. Hardly anyone believed these guys were crazy enough to do something like that. Nobody sets fire to farts. This was all a bunch of baloney. Why, hell, these were grown men.

Knobby heard and he believed.

10 Henrietta And the Honey Hole

If Henrietta Schwartzkopf wasn't the fattest woman around, she was certainly a close second. Nobody at Knobby's could overlook her, and if they were not fortunate enough to cast their eyes upon this jiggling, jaggling, wiggling, waggling undulation of corpulence, they most assuredly heard stories about this rather fleshy female.

To watch Henrietta get into a boat was one of the most thrilling and amusing experiences anyone could have without actually participating in the activity. She was so fat she couldn't raise one leg high enough to get it over the gunwhale. What she did was to sit on the gunwhale and slowly squirm her buttocks onto the seat, then lean back and while grunting and groaning raise one leg then the other into the boat. This event took about thirty minutes to accomplish. And all this had to be done from shore. She could not and would not enter the boat from a dock because she could not control her balance and the boat would pitch perilously to the point of capsizing.

Once Henrietta was settled in the boat whoever was with her would rev up the motor, then Ralph and some others would push and rock the boat out into deeper water until the motor could take over. When returning from fishing the same comedy would be replayed. People in camp discreetly hung around to see how she would maneuver the 300 pounds out of the boat. The boat would come into shore at full speed so Henrietta would have some solid ground under her when wiggling out of the boat. There were times when the boat hit the shore so hard it almost propelled her out. "Not so fast, you dummy," she would shout as she tried to rearrange her weight.

One thing about Henrietta, she had enough sense to wear the right kind of clothes. Slacks and a button-down-the-front type jacket. Looked from the back like Two Ton Tony. Then all that attire was set off with a floppy hat she tied under the area that would be designated as her chin. The folds of her skin angled directly from her lower lip to her chest. It was like watching a ripple effect with her flesh falling from her chin, oscillating its way toward the mid-section, and coming to rest around her lower abdomen.

A little more background on Henrietta and how she became part of Knobby's contingency. Besides being fat she was also very rich. She came from the long line of the Eickbush family that cleared hundreds and hundreds of acres to the south and settled in to stay family after family. The Eickbushes were thick as thieves, and some even suspicioned the latter, one of the largest landowners in the state, and ultra conservative with their money. As an example, the Matriarch Eickbush bought toilet paper in bulk directly from the paper mills. They were primarily dairy farmers with large herds of Holsteins and Guernseys. They were also entrepreneurs with operations going beyond just milk and cheese production.

They distributed dairy processing equipment throughout a multi-state region, operated a fleet of trucks, and owned a string of retail outlets called "Bush's" where you could buy most anything from blood pudding to ice cream. They were very rich and very much family. All the kinfolk worked in the business.

It had become difficult to get Henrietta married off because even at an early age she was overly plump. After years of trying the ruling Eickbush finally found John Schwartzkopf. The dowry was a large parcel of land and plenty of dairy cattle for starters. Problem with this arrangement was apparent from the beginning. John gave dairy farming only a passive effort. He liked to go fishing too much. And the two of them couldn't produce a family to the chagrin of Patriarch Eickbush. "Familie ist familie," the ruling elder would proclaim.

John, and a buddy of his by the name of Walt Zuckschwerdt, would take off for Knobby's about three or four times during the season on what John called "speed runs" and "weekend missions". Each time he returned to the farm and Henrietta he was full of energy and enthusiasm. A good fisherman, he usually brought back enough catch for several meals but with Henrietta's appetite, the fish were soon gone. Then, when John's physical batteries would begin to get run down, he would give Zucky a call. "Ready for another speed run next weekend?" Zucky was unmarried and always ready to go fishing.

Henrietta never looked favorably on all this since she thought the two of them were after more than fish. "John, if I find out there's hanky-panky going on up there, I'll have your head on that butchering block."

John, of course, denied any such thing as she presumed and off he would go. The next time he made ready to go fishing, however, Henrietta intervened and said, "You better get used to me going with you, John, 'cause from now on I'm your fishing partner."

There was little he could do. If he wanted to fish, Henrietta had to go along. Any refusal on his part brought a terse rebuttal from Henrietta. "You want Papa to know what's going on?" And John didn't.

The first trip the two of them made to Knobby's the weather was miserable. Rainy, and cold. John surely had planned it this way and Henrietta did not go out fishing. But she seemed to enjoy herself sitting in the cabin constantly nibbling on foodstuffs and reading romantic novels. On their next few fishing trips she continued staying in the cabin while John fished the time away. It was the night John didn't return that Henrietta became worried, excited, and skeptical about where John was fishing. She found Knobby in the Lounge.

"John hasn't come in yet and I'm worried," she said loudly and nervously.

"Oh, I wouldn't be too concerned. John knows the lake well and maybe he's found a honey hole," Knobby replied. "Besides he fishes at night a lot."

Well, Henrietta didn't like the tone of that remark at all. "I want you to go out and look for him."

"Don't worry, Mrs. Schwartzkopf, he's okay."

Henrietta stormed out of the Lounge and waddled to the dock where she bellowed, "John—John—John." Lights went on in several of the cabins as the shouts of "John—John—John" got louder. Knobby had to go down there and reassure her that John would return shortly. John finally did at six the next morning and found Henrietta up and packed and boiling mad. "We're leaving right now," she fumed.

As their big Chrysler pulled away you could see Henrietta sitting in the back seat snapping and pointing her finger at John. "Wait 'til Papa hears about this."

In all probability Papa did hear about John's prolonged

absence but quite unfortunately John fell victim to a stampede of Holsteins that trampled and jostled his body lifeless.

Two years later Henrietta returned to Knobby's sitting in the rear seat of that same big Chrysler. This time it was chauffeured by Walt Zuckschwerdt. Apparently, the elder Eickbush got to Zucky and offered him all kinds of amenities if only he would take Henrietta away from the farm for a week and go fishing with her. Bear in mind that Henrietta had never actually gone fishing during the times she came with John. She just stayed in the cabin. Well, the week she came up with Zucky was one week worth talking about and one in which Knobby and the gang almost picked up stakes and left for parts unknown.

First, Zucky had to get her in the boat which he finally did displaying a type of patience reserved primarily for Popes, Bishops, and other assorted Holy Men. Once out on the water they traveled with the bow of the boat slanting down. Whenever they hit a small swale, the motor would rise out of the water and whirr loudly.

"Now, don't move until I tell you," Zucky told her.

"When do I start fishing?" she asked.

"When I tell you," Zucky replied as he gunned the ten horsepower motor as fast as it would take them across the water to an out-of-the-way bay in quiet waters where they would not be seen.

"Do I fish now?"

Zucky put a nightcrawler on her hook and tossed the line in the water. "When you feel the line get tight and feel some jerks, you got a fish. Then, just raise the rod and reel the line in by cranking the handle," he explained. "You got all that?"

He eased his back against the motor and contemplated why he ever agreed to going on trial like this, and sharply recalled the words of elder Eickbush. "You will be handsomely rewarded."

Just then Henrietta heaved her massive body backwards mightily raising the fishing rod and flipping a palm-size perch clean out of the water skyward. It smacked the water behind her.

"I got one!" she yelled.

Zucky had to explain to her that strength wasn't necessary, that touch and deftness would work better. But several more perch were rocketed out of the water and seen heading for the puffy cumulus. Each time that would happen the boat would lurch so abruptly that everything in the bottom slid dangerously close to the gunwhale. It was all Zucky could do to counterweight the reaction. Fortunately, only a little water slopped in, and oddly Henrietta seemed unconcerned about the risk.

"This fishing is fun," she exclaimed.

"I should have brought a butterfly net."

"Let's go to another place."

"Don't move," Zucky shouted. "It's time to go in."

After they unloaded Zucky headed for the Lounge and, after steadying his now exasperated nervous system with several straight shots of whiskey, he told the group seated there the events of the afternoon.

"And now she says she likes fishing," he commented.

When he got back to the cabin Henrietta had a mess of bluegills deep frying for dinner.

"Where'd these come from?"

"I bought them from the group in the next cabin," she said.

This would be the Polishers who kept everything they caught and were not opposed to selling most anything they had available.

Henrietta by now was enjoying the art of fishing and was becoming better at bringing them into the boat. But all the while Zucky was paying a very stiff emotional price to endure the experience. He was a nervous wreck eating less and drinking more. One night after another purchased fish dinner he zonked out in his bed oblivious to anything. Henrietta, meanwhile, was in good spirits so she headed for the Lounge for a few nightcaps and conversation about her fishing prowess.

"Where's Knobby?" she hollered upon entering. "I want to tell him about all the fish I caught."

All the eyes of those seated at the bar focused on the tent-shaped form that found a single chair and overwhelmed it. Women didn't normally take over the sanctity of this Lounge with the sort of bravado she displayed, but the men had no aspirations of trying to remove Henrietta and were more inclined to let her stay after she offered, "Ralph, set up the boys. This round's on me."

And so were all of the rest of the rounds, for that matter. Henrietta finally had Ralph hand her the bottle of Schnapps which she held on her lap and poured with uncontrolled regularity into a shot glass that looked like a thimble in her puffy hand.

"Where's Knobby?" she sing-songed. "I gotta tell old Knob about de fishies I caught."

Just as dramatically as she entered, Henrietta forced herself out the door with a waggle that fortunately prevented her from teetering over. She headed for Knobby's cabin which she spotted easily enough with the help of a full moon. Knobby was fast asleep but not in such a deep slumber that he couldn't hear some noise on the porch. It sounded guttural. "Knoobeee." He got out of bed and looked toward his front door. There stood a large figure outlined by the moonlight. Its arms spraddled the doorway, steadying that body against the outside wall. Its thick head rose and deeply yelled, "Knoobeee."

"What the hell is that!" he asked himself. His first premonition was that it was one of those big black bears that hung around the garbage dump. He went into his kitchen and grabbed two large saucepans. He eased himself near the front door then sharply banged the pans together and yelled, "Skeedat, Skeedat, Skeedat" as loud as he could. You could even hear the noise in the Lounge and some of those that were still there ambled out to see what was happening. What they saw was Henrietta high-tailing it down the path grunting and gasping toward her cabin as fast as her stubby legs could take her.

The following day Zucky heard what happened and laughed uproariously with the others about how the big black female bear tried to put the moves on Knobby.

Oddly enough, that didn't slow Henrietta down one tad. She and Zucky went out fishing again and still his teachings hadn't improved her skill to much degree. It was still pull as hard as she could and "smack" the poor fish would be flattened on the water behind her. When they returned, Zucky headed for the Lounge. Henrietta bought some more fish from the Polishers. After dinner Zucky again fell victim to a deep alcohol induced slumber, and Henrietta headed for the Lounge. Knobby was tending bar and growled to himself as she draped her body around the weakened chair.

"Knoobeee," she crooned. "The drinks are on me and I'll take the bottle of Schnapps."

The usual group was more talkative than the previous night asking Henrietta what she was catching, what she was using, and where all this was happening.

"Zucky says I'm catching goggle-eyed perch. He puts a worm on the hook and I haul 'em in."

The usual group nodded agreeingly and made small talk about how good she was getting. Old Sam the Chummer said, "Your departed husband would be proud of you."

Henrietta, now giddy from the Schnapps, tried to reply by commenting, "I'm gonna get a whopper tomorrow 'cause I'm telling Zucky to take me to John's favorite honey hole." The usual group looked warily at each other.

The next day the odd couple went out fishing again with Henrietta insisting that they go to John's favorite "honey hole." Zucky motored their boat to the far end of the lake and told Henrietta that the wind was just right for drifting and that they would find the "honey hole" somewhere out there in the deepest part of the lake. Actually, Zucky was plain worn out and wanted more to rest this way than to have his body rocked back and forth as Henrietta was catching perch.

"I'm putting this big minnow on your hook and this lead weight," he told her. "Now you let out a lot of line so the minnow will go to the bottom."

"Are there fish around here?"

"You bet there are," Zucky replied. "This is how you find the honey hole, but you got to sit still, then when your line gets tight you pull hard and reel it in."

The drift was perfect and Zucky dozed, occasionally resting against the motor. Henrietta was as still as a churchmouse watching her line slanting in the water.

"When am I going to catch a fish?"

"You have to be patient when fishing for big fish. Just keep doing what you're doing."

"Are there really big fish here?" she asked.

"You bet there are. Monsters like what's on the wall in the Lounge."

Henrietta became more intense at watching her line and Zucky became more relaxed. Some minutes later his serenity was interrupted.

"My line is dragging on something."

Zucky opened his eyes and sure enough Henrietta's line was tight and the rod tip bent toward the water. "Pull up on the rod and see what happens," he said.

She did and seemed to move whatever was on the end of the hook.

"Pull harder," Zucky yelled, "and reel in some line."

She did and was able to bring in some line but whenever Henrietta eased up, down the rod would go, and she would have to loosen her grip on the reel handle.

"Looks to me like you got your hands full with one of those monster pikes or even a wandering sturgeon that hang out around here. Pull up hard," he said, "and see what happens."

She did and her massive body slouched against the side of the boat. Her rod tip waved up and down. "Reel in some line," Zucky yelled.

She reeled in some line but after a few feet down again the line would go and Henrietta pulled harder on the rod. She was not about to give in to this fish and by now she had the butt of the rod pressed into her mid-section where her navel may have been. For what seemed to be several minutes Henrietta would raise up on the rod, reel in some more line, then pump the rod again. Whenever she relaxed her grip, however, the monster fish had other thoughts and down into the depths it would go.

"Keep at it!" Zucky yelled. "Don't let it get away."

Now Henrietta was sweating profusely and had a pulse rate heading for 200. Other boats in the area saw the action and came closer to watch Henrietta handle this fish. Some of the enthusiastic ones in the audience hollered encouragement.

"Let it run."

"Loosen your drag."

"Have you set the hook?"

"What are you using?"

Zucky said, "Don't listen to all that crap. You just keep pulling and reeling and I'll help you get the fish in."

Henrietta was panting and gasping for breath working as hard as she could to get the fish up. "This is a helluva honey hole," she grunted. She took a deep breath and put all of her upper weight behind pulling up the rod. As she reeled in more line bubbles surged up and the water appeared agitated.

"You got it now," someone yelled.

Zucky had the landing net ready. Henrietta reared backwards, her eyes fixed heavenward and pulled with every effort she had left. She reeled fast until the surface of the water splashed open.

"My God," Zucky exclaimed. "You caught yourself a king-size cedar tree."

The top of an old cedar tree came out of the water. It was held firmly by the line entwined in its branches and bounced with the undulations of the lake. Applause came from some of the boats.

"Good job."

"Nice catch."

"It's a keeper."

Henrietta was spent, exhausted, bent over gasping for breath. Before Zucky could do anything she loosened her grip on the rod and the king-size cedar tree dove to the bottom taking the rod with it. The handle of the rod hit Henrietta on one of her chins and out she went.

"My God," Zucky squealed. "I gotta get her back. She's passed out."

Some of the lighter, faster boats sped back to Knobby's to

alert those around shore that Henrietta had an accident and would need help. By the time Zucky pulled in there was a goodly crowd. He slammed into shore. Henrietta's limp body was spread throughout the front of the boat.

"We got to bring her to," said Sam the Chummer.

"Knobby, you know mouth-to-mouth," Mac McFarland exclaimed. "Go to work on her."

"Slap her wrists," said Marge.

"Maybe we ought to get her outta the boat first," Little Joe remarked. That comment apparently fell on deaf ears.

"I'm not going to give her mouth-to-mouth," Knobby stated. "Where's Ralph?"

"He'll get her drunk," someone said. Ralph was part of the original crowd but edged away when mouth-to-mouth was suggested. Instead he got a large pail and dipped into the water.

"Clear the way," he yelled. "I'll bring her around."

The cold water hit Henrietta full in the face. She shook uncontrollably, then opened her eyes and took a long deep breath of air then puffed it out with her cheeks. Her pale color gave into pink then red. She heaved her body more erect on the boat seat and looked at the crowd that had gathered.

"That was sure one helluva honey hole," she said. "Now where's my fish?"

11  Tarts for Sale

Nobody could spend much time around Knobby's without hearing about the scrumptious homemade pies that could be bought at some woman's house about six miles from camp. Hearing about her pies was appetizing enough but tasting them was an experience reserved for the likes of Kings and Queens. Apple, cherry, strawberry, blueberry, butterscotch, pecan, banana cream, rhubarb, pumpkin, boysenberry, gooseberry, peach. You name it and Delores Duval could make it better than those kinds of delicacies served in the finest restaurants around the world.

Besides having a reputation for delicious homemade pies Delores (she's better known around these parts as DeeDee) also discreetly ran a small bar in the living room of her home. "Ran" is probably the right word but more often it was referred to as "she managed to make available a drink or two from her personal stock for a mere stipend." The fact that her personal supply of liquor was more than some of the pubs in town was never publicized to much extent.

Another thing DeeDee specialized in was making available, depending on one's craving, tarts to go with her pies.

First, a little background on DeeDee. Maybe you recall reading or hearing about the Duval River, one of the tributaries that helped to produce the entire water system here, and the young Duval daughter who was seduced by the Shaughnessey kid. Well, the girl was Delores Duval and the family shipped her away to spend the rest of her life with her aunt who lived miles away in the western part of the state. The aunt ran the finest bawdy house in the state and apparently none of the other family members were aware of this. All they knew was that Aunt Marie was very well off, widowed, and highly respected.

Those formidable years DeeDee spent with Aunt Marie quickly molded the demur Duval daughter into a paramour beyond compare. Developing from an adolescent teenage temptress to a coveted lady of the night, DeeDee learned the trade of her tricks quite well. Even the Marquise de Pompadour would have been envious. Her reputation grew and her expertise was known throughout most of the country.

It wasn't too long until a wealthy timber baron took a liking to DeeDee. It didn't matter that he was married, a leading philanthropist, church elder, thirty-third degree mason, political powerhouse. He had to have DeeDee for his very own. So, he agreed to pay Aunt Marie a healthy sum along with a guarantee, like a perpetual trust, that she could stay in business forever. Then he established DeeDee in her own home where he would be the only overnight visitor. This worked well for many years. DeeDee was more than satisfied with the financial arrangement and he was satisfied with his bed partner. All this came to a halt when the millionaire was nominated to run for senator. Not only did his wife tell him it was time to stop fooling around but even the bigwigs in Washington told him to keep things zipped up or his chances for political success would be squelched.

He settled up with DeeDee to the tune of, some reports have it, close to a million dollars. He paid dearly for his years of pleasure but all this was not public knowledge elsewhere in the state, and especially around Knobby's. Oh, sure, Knobby and a few of the others knew about her background and more than a few eyebrows were raised when DeeDee bought the ranch type bungalow nestled in the woods just off the county road. Her move was all very quiet. Some said she paid cash for the house and the forty acres that came with it, including a four acre pond.

Many wondered whether DeeDee would be content to live by herself in the woods after all those years of promiscuity. None wondered more than Jailer John. He made it a point to check periodically about how she was adjusting to the life of seclusion. Jailer John had his eye on not only DeeDee but also on the pond in the back of her property that supposedly had the biggest bass in the entire state living in its waters. Stories about the Killer Bass had circulated around here for years but the previous owners never allowed anyone to fish the pond. The Jailer thought he could get the job done by sidling up to DeeDee and keeping her on the right side of the law.

For a long time DeeDee behaved herself and cultivated her pie making talents. The first anyone knew about her pies was when she put up a sign by the road leading to her place that read "HOMEMADE PIES FOR SALE." Then little by little her reputation as a piemaker grew in the same proportion as her former vocation.

Shortly after the sign went up, DeeDee made some modifications to her home. She completely redid the living room and made it into what could be considered as a domesticated cocktail lounge. It was still a living room with the usual sofa, easy chairs, and table, radio, etc . . ., but it was also big enough to accommodate some small tables and chairs. She also had a small wet bar constructed and placed just inside the front door. DeeDee could be found most of the time behind the bar reading a newspaper, a book, working crossword puzzles, sipping on some sour mash, and constantly sucking on a cigarette.

During the alterations to the living room, she also had everything redone in a pale pink—walls, ceiling, lampshades, drapes, doors. And somehow the paint must have contained an overriding aroma of perfume. But she could sure make good pies so nobody said much about her color scheme or the sweet, sexy smell.

It didn't take long for some of Knobby's regulars to start showing up at DeeDee's for pie, coffee, and other liquid refreshments. Then the card games would start: pinochle, hearts, high-low-jick-jack-and game, euchre, poker. Moose Weinantz was the best at every game and let everyone know this.

"Three of a kind. Pot's mine," you would hear him yell.

Jailer John was always around trying to get close to DeeDee and her pond in the back so he didn't try to enforce much law. All he would say was, "Keep the money off the table, men. I don't want the state gendarmes closing this place down."

"How you expect us to bet?" asked Ralph.

"Use matches," replied Jailer John.

"Whatta he say," asked Sam the Chummer.

"You're not in the game," Moose yelled, "so sit still and have another piece of pie."

The Jailer leaned against the small bar and looked at DeeDee. Through the years her marketing of pleasure had taken its toll. Her pale face sagged in wrinkles. Her eye sockets were puffed and framed glassy unfocusing eyes. Make up was a major part of her complexion. Her salt and pepper patched hair was unmanageable. And her hacking cough would bring an immediate invitation from any tuberculosis sanitarium.

"I'll have an easy rye," said Jailer.

DeeDee acknowledged with a *"Haaawwwk. Haaawwwk. Coming right up."*

It wouldn't be surprising if some of her cigarette ash didn't drop in the glass. The thin white cylinder of tobacco never left her lips.

"DeeDee," Jailer said, "when you and I gonna go fishing in your pond?"

"Those fish aren't doing any harm," she said. "Let them live in peace."

"Yeah, but how about that lunker bass you got out there?" Jailer remarked. "I could catch that, have it mounted, and put it up here on your wall."

"I'm sure that's not the only thing you want to mount," DeeDee replied smartly.

"That bass is the biggest bass in the state," he said without reacting to her comment. "You could be famous."

"I've had enough fame for a lifetime."

"Why don't you let me wet a line out there one of these days."

DeeDee handed him the glass of rye and with a teasing look of yesteryear said, "We'll see," then she went into her *"Haaawwwk. Haaawwwk."*

Most of DeeDee Duval's affection was directed to her overweight, blind basset hound. It was aging only slightly faster than she. Blackie was its name and it rested on top of one end of the bar and moved only when it felt a wandering cockroach or when it detected a conflict in its master's voice. The tone of her hacking cough prompted Blackie to waddle down the bar to where it nudged Jailer John on his arm. It kept nudging until Jailer moved away. Moose Weinantz saw and heard what was going on at the bar and yelled, "John, that dog's got your number. Give old Blackie a sip of your rye and he'll see that you fish that pond."

"If you don't watch it," Jailer blurted out, "I'll close this place down."

Just then Blackie jumped down from the bar and headed for the door. "Jimmy's coming," said DeeDee.

Nobody, of course, heard anything what with the level of conversation, but old Blackie could hear the Model A engine purring miles away. And sure enough soon in came Jimmy Murphy. Blackie jumped up on him until Jimmy reached in his coat pocket and pulled out a carmel candy. The dog gulped it down and begged for more. Jimmy sat down in the easy chair by the bar and doled out more carmels to Blackie. DeeDee gave Jimmy a whiskey.

"Rough night?" she asked. She asked him again a couple of octaves higher, "ROUGH NIGHT?"

"Oh, yes. The Lantern Inn was full up. Sophie at the Vagabond isn't feeling good. And Cappelleti is thinking about selling out."

"That's too bad."

Jimmy Murphy was a railroad brakeman and every Friday night he would drive from town and stop at every roadhouse, bar, salon, inn, tavern on the right hand side of the road until he got to DeeDee's. He had one drink at each stop so you could count on him having a goodly snoot full by the time he arrived. He was pushing retirement age but looked like he had passed that years ago. The weather, coal soot, long hours, and his whisky had done the job. After two drinks at DeeDee's, because he had to stay longer in order to feed Blackie, he would head back to town and stop at every watering hole on that side of the road. Jimmy had been doing this every Friday night for years and you could almost set your watch to his arrival.

"You still got your eye on that Killer Bass out there?" he asked Jailer.

"I'd sure like to set my hook in that old codger," the Jailer replied. "You know it's gotta be a state record."

"One time," Jimmy said, "I saw that bass go for a frog and it jumped so high out of the water it hit a limb on an oak tree and knocked a squirrel out of its nest and into the water."

"Shut him off," Moose yelled.

"Know why that bass's so big?" Jimmy asked.

All eyes in her living room turned toward Jimmy sitting in the easy chair and feeding caramels to Blackie.

" 'Cause DeeDee here chums that pond of hers with left-over pies. I saw that bass handle a pie in one gulp. Ain't that right, DeeDee?"

"Wrong, Jimmy," she answered. "I use a mixture of potato peels and whiskey. That's why he's so fat."

"Just keep this dog away from shore," Jimmy said. "He'd make a tasty meal for old Killer."

"You've had enough, Jimmy," she said, " 'Bout time you headed back."

All this conversation stimulated Jailer John's imagination of hooking into the Killer Bass.

It was when DeeDee replaced her "HOMEMADE PIES FOR SALE" sign and put up another that read "TARTS FOR SALE" that she started to test the thin thread of legality in the area. Two of her former girlfriends from Aunt Marie's just happened to drop in for the weekend. They were living legends of the bawdy house days still plying their wares to whomever was in the market. After a couple of weeks in the woods and on the water DeeDee thought there would be a few sportsmen interested in enjoying feminine pleasures. The two ladies would quietly saunter around the living room watching the card games and getting refills for the gentlemen. Moose Weinantz took a shine to one of them.

"Deal me out of this pot," he yelled. "I'm going to see if DeeDee's tarts are as good as her pies."

"Whatta he say?" asked Sam.

"He's checking the tarts," said Ralph.

"Someone fart?" asked Sam.

The two ladies hung around for a couple of months with DeeDee alternating the "PIE" and "TART" signs outside her place. The women added an element of intrigue to DeeDees. They also added some leverage for Jailer John.

"DeeDee," he said. "You can't have these women here doing what it is they're doing. It's bad enough your selling drinks without a license. I may have to enforce the law."

"They're just a couple of friends of mine," she said, "that are passing through until they get relocated."

"Well, if the gendarmes find out about this, you could be in hot water," Jailer John remarked. "Me too, for that matter."

"Speaking of water, John, how would you like to fish for that bass next Sunday?" she asked.

Jailer John forgot all about enforcing the law and replied, "I may need more than one day to catch that fish."

"And my two lady friends may need to stay here all summer and on into fall until they get relocated," DeeDee commented.

"Well, I'll see what can be worked out," Jailer said, "but take that 'TARTS FOR SALE' sign down. People are starting to ask me questions."

"I've got homemade tarts available that are just as good as the pies." DeeDee snapped. "You've tried them."

"They're good all right," Jailer said, "but it's the women I'm concerned about."

"You leave that to me, John," said DeeDee. "Now what about Sunday? You want to fish the pond?"

"You bet your sweet ass I do."

"I'll chum that bass for the next few days," she said, "so he'll be ready for you."

All John could think about was looking forward to Sunday and fishing for that bass. He went over his lures, relined his

reel, and mentally imagined how he would attack the Killer Bass. DeeDee had a johnboat that he could use and he envisioned working the entire shoreline until he found his prey.

Bright and early Sunday morning Jailer John was out on the pond. For hours he tossed Jitterbugs, Hula Poppers, Buzz Baits, pork rind, rubber worms almost everything he had in his tackle box but he could not stimulate old Killer Bass. All John did was make that bass madder by the moment. After a few days of DeeDee's chumming mixture that bass wanted peace and quiet on a Sunday morning. Jailer John was not about to concede to that.

What happened to John was actually documented by DeeDee and the two women who saw John in the boat out on the pond. The first thing they said they noticed was the boat moving in a circle without John touching the oars. John was waving his arms then holding on to the sides of the boat. Killer Bass had taken hold of the anchor rope and was moving the boat around in circles.

The next thing that happened to Jailer John was he was being pitched up and down in the boat by that bass forcing itself against the underside of the boat. The more John was jostled the more the johnboat took in water and slowly submerged. Jailer John jumped out near some cattails and raced through the shallow water for shore. From what the women said he turned and saw Killer Bass leaping from the water after him. The Jailer thrashed through the reeds and floundered up on shore. He saw the huge bass open its large mouth and let out a noise that sounded like a loud burp then it flopped back into the water and lazily finned its way to deeper sanctity.

Of course, Jailer John told a different story about how he hooked the bass and fought it for an hour or more until his line broke. He said he never saw a bass so big and mean which was the only truth to this escapade.

DeeDee's two lady friends finally left but she still put out the "TARTS FOR SALE" sign whenever she had the delicacies available. She continued making pies and people from all over would drop by to purchase some. She also continued to serve drinks in her living room and whenever Jailer John cautioned her about this she would say, "You don't want those men to hear what really happened with you and Killer Bass do you?"

Blackie died and DeeDee had a regular funeral for him. He was buried in the woods and the men placed a large rock over his grave. Every Saturday morning the chipmunks and squirrels would fight over the caramel candies they found on the rock.

12 Shave and A Haircut: Eight Bits

One of the nicest persons you could ever meet, whether it be at Knobby's or not, was Willis "Pops" Robertson. He was even-tempered, mild mannered, unlike most of the rambunctious regulars at this fishing camp.

If you saw him walking around camp at any time of day, it was always a wide smile and either a "hello," "good morning," "good day," "how are ya," "nice seeing ya." A genuine Mister Nice Guy. Pops, however, never socialized much and kept to himself which meant that his friendly manner wasn't shared all the time. He always stayed in the smallest cabin Knobby had. This would be Vagabond, nestled among some pine trees near the main dock. Pops was here from opening day in May until October so you were certain to run into him and be exposed to his congeniality, but he preferred his solitude and rarely congregated in the Lounge or with others in their cabins.

Pops was a retired barber. Used to have a barber shop

across the state line which was called "Pops' Palace." It had four chairs but most waited for Pops because he took the extra time for the massaging and soothing that made haircuts worth waiting for. For over thirty years he barbered and his stature showed it. Much like doctors and dentists he was stooped over with what is called a Dowager's Hump, and he walked rather gingerly with short steps. This must have been the result of standing on his feet all those hours for all those years.

Pops was so thin he would shuffle backwards when he sneezed. He was bald like a lot of barbers but had plenty of hair on his upper lip. Wire frame glasses set off his squinty eyes that came from smiling all the time. His constant smile exposed perfect white teeth which were his very own.

The first time Pops ever came to Knobby's was years ago when Doctor DuCette brought him here for opening day. The doctor was one of his customers and knew Pops' interest in fishing. Pops was widowed and his family scattered all over the country so when he retired he decided to spend six months of the year fishing the system at Lake of Six Rivers.

The interesting thing about Pops was that he fished only for bluegills. He absolutely refused to go after walleyes, northerns, perch, bass, and would not keep these fish if they came upon his bait. Ralph claims he actually saw Pops bring in a perch and a large northern struck into it. The northern hung tight, moved the boat around, thrashed the water, but rather than play the northern Pops cut the line. Ralph said the northern would have been trophy size.

Pops fished every available day, rain or shine, and unless storm warnings were out with gale winds whipping up whitecaps, you knew he would be out there anchored over one of his "quiet spots," as he called them, fishing for bluegills. Pops fished with two cane poles, bobbers, and used only red worms. He knew every weed bed in the water system and would anchor over it, magically flipping those cane poles in a way that dropped the worm ladened hook into the water with hardly a splash. "Bluegills are flighty," he would say. "You never want to scare 'em away."

Then when the red and white bobber dipped under the water Pops would just as deftly raise the cane pole almost effortlessly and bring in a bluegill. He fished as unperturbably as his on shore behavior. Seeing Pops out there fishing was like viewing a Monet painting or reading a Walt Whitman poem. Only on a few occasions did anything upset Pops, but once it did his Scottish bile riled up into a cutting and unforgiving anger.

The good part about all his bluegill fishing was that once a month on a Friday night Knobby would have an all-you-can-eat fish fry courtesy of Pops. Pops prepared and fried the bluegills along with his special fried potatoes and onions. Anyone in camp, if they wanted to, could come to the fish fry for free. All they had to pay for was their liquid refreshments. Some people used to plan their fishing trips so they would be there on the last Friday of the month for Pops' famous fish fry. Nobody ever took extra advantage of the all-you-can-eat menu except the Polishers. They gobbled up the bluegills as if they had fasted for a week. And if there were any left they would ask for them for their next meal. This never bothered Pops as long as everyone enjoyed the bluegills which they certainly did.

Besides doing the bluegill fry every month, Pops also provided shaves and haircuts in his cabin. This service wasn't advertised widely since Pops really didn't want to get back in the business again, but for Knobby, Sam, Ralph, and a few others he would freely render his skills. For others he would charge one dollar. Can you imagine a hot towel, smooth shave, and a neat trim for only a dollar. All this and some gentle talk on the art of bluegill fishing. The fee "kept him in red worms," as he would say.

"Bluegills like quiet waters," Pops said trimming Ralph's sideburns one day. "So you gotta be quiet also."

"You're right."

"No fussin' around in the boat," Pops continued. "Need to be as still as a churchmouse."

"Yup."

"Need the touch of a surgeon also. Once you feel their little mouth sucking up that worm," Pops went on, "then apply some slight pressure on the line."

"You're right."

"It's done in one motion," Pops said. Working the scissors around Ralph's ear. "No hard pulling. Just a feel and pop the tip."

"Yup."

"How about going out with me tomorrow, Ralph? I'll show you how it's done."

"Can't make it," Ralph replied. "Knobby's got me fixin' one of the motors."

The only person probably closest to Pops was Sam the Chummer. The reason being was that both of them had a compulsion toward crossword puzzles. They competed against each other to see who could finish a puzzle in the fastest time. And if one ever was stumped on a word, it would delight the other to provide the correct word. They even checked each other's completed puzzle to see if there were any errors or convenient make believe words. Sam was the champ and would always gloat, "When you can use a pen to work yours, Pops, then you can really challenge me."

One time Big Joe was sitting in the stiff back chair with a towel wrapped over his shoulders and Pops was working on the hair on the back of his neck. He had lowered Big Joe's head so he could snip the smaller but pesty hairs there. All you could hear was the *clik, clik, clik,* of the scissors until the door of the Vagabond cabin was shoved open.

"I finally got 56 Across," yelled Sam.

With that Big Joe jolted back and Pops snipped a wide swatch of hair from the back of his head. Big Joe yelled back, "You idiot! What if he had a razor in his hand?"

Sam paid no attention and said, "Remember 56 Across yesterday? Three letter word for Jungfrau."

"Yes," Pops replied. "That's ALP."

"Well, you smart ass, you," and Sam stormed out.

Big Joe also got his shave and haircut free since he made the beautiful sign that Pops displayed over the kitchen sink. "POPS' TONSORIAL PARLOR" it read and was edged with ornate designs depicting the barbering trade. But Big Joe must have been jinxed getting his hair cut by Pops. Another time when Pops had just finished shaving the underside of his chin, the group in the next cabin walked by and held up two stringers of bluegills. Pops told Big Joe to rest easy and he went outside to see the mess.

"They're almost jumping in the boat around the stick ups," the neighbor said.

That was all Pops needed. He toweled off Big Joe and told him to come back tomorrow so he could finish off the shave. Then he went out fishing for bluegills for the rest of the afternoon.

Generally, everyone knew Pops was easy-going and that it took a lot to get his dander up but when it happened, watch out. One day Pops had been out fishing all morning in a quiet bay and doing quite well with the bluegills. Some fisherman roared by the inlet at full speed throwing up a wake that thrashed against the shoreline and rocked everything in Pops' boat. Pops turned in time to see the man speeding by with his long blonde hair flowing in the breeze. As soon as the water calmed the same boat raced back again past the inlet then zigzagged in the open water jumping across the watery furrows.

Hot rodding on these waters was a no-no but occasionally there was the oddball who got his thrills by trying to get by with unacceptable behavior. Pops was madder than a hornet and headed in. He stopped to see Knobby and told him about the incident out on the water and wondered who the man was. Knobby said he would check into it.

Pops finished his lunch, worked on his crossword puzzle, then napped, still smarting about that young man with the blonde hair. A knock on his cabin door awoke him. He went to the door and there stood the blonde haired speedboater.

"Knobby said you might be able to give me a shave and haircut."

Pops clenched his perfect white teeth and restrained himself from lashing out vocally and maybe physically, then deviously invited the young man inside.

"You say Knobby told you I give haircuts?"

"Yeah, I have to leave tonight 'cause I'm meeting my girlfriend's family tomorrow. We're planning to get married and I want to look sharp for my new in-laws."

"Well, a shave and a haircut will fix you up."

"Just a trim will be fine."

To make a long story short Pops did a job on that young man's hair that would have been the envy of a Mohawk Indian. The shears cut a deep swath up and around the back of his head. Then Pops started along the sides.

"Don't take too much off," the young man said. The damage, however, had already been done.

"I'm thinning some off the back and sides so you'll be able to groom it better."

"Feels like you're taking too much off," he said. "Where's your mirror?"

"I'll get it for you when I'm done," replied Pops. "You'll be able to see the finished product then."

Pops continued shearing and snipping here and there then wetted the hair down. He fluffed it dry then combed the remains.

"There, that should make your new in-laws stand up and take notice," said Pops removing the towel. "Since you've got a special occasion coming up, the haircut's on the house."

Pops handed the young man the mirror. He looked at himself in the mirror and screamed. "My God! You've scalped me! What the hell you think you're doing?" He continued looking at himself in the mirror and yelling at Pops. "This is rotten. You call yourself a barber? You're a butcher. I'll have your ass for this."

As the young man with the new shorn blonde hair turned to go after Pops all he saw in front of him was the straight razor Pops held in his hand. It moved back and forth like a cobra's head then the razor pointed to the door. "Out," Pops demanded, "and don't come back."

The young man and his new hair-do stomped out the door covering his head with his hands as he rushed away.

That night Pops went to Knobby's Lounge for one of his infrequent visits. He was all smiles and ordered a soft drink.

"Hope you didn't mind my sending some young kid to your place for a haircut," Knobby said with a wide grin.

"Not at all," Pops replied.

13 | The Polish Express

When the Polishers arrived in camp they did so in style. An old school bus that they had converted into a Pullmanette on wheels would come bouncing its way down the narrow lane and past the various cabins. Most of the bus was still in its original yellow color but the Polishers had added broad red stripes along the top and bottom. One of the Polishers must have hand lettered the wording, "The Polish Express" on both sides. It was painted over the school township designation but they left the figure No. 12. Big Joe Runyon swore he had nothing to do with the graphics scheme and didn't want any part of improving it.

The yellow and red bus was not the only signal that the Polishers had arrived. You could tell a week before they got here that they were coming because Knobby was at his grumpiest best. Once they pulled in he would storm about getting upset at almost anything.

He was always on hand to greet them. "You guys keep that bus next to the cabin," he told them. "I don't want it parked in front or out on the road."

Then he would walk away from whomever of the Polishers he was yelling at and continue hollering about something. "And I don't want anymore cleaning fish in the cabin."

The Polish Express had the original driver's seat and the two bench seats behind it. After that they had rigged up bunk beds, two on a side to sleep four. Nine people usually made the trip in reasonably comfortable style. The rest of the bus carried enough food to stock an all-night mini-mart, all their fishing gear, and a lot of flat corrugated cartons. When they got out of the bus it was Graminski, Walorski, Laskowski, Malinski, Bielawski, Sobrieski, Pulaski, Wendowski, Krakowski, and not necessarily in that order. There were more skis than at a Winter Olympics downhill event. They were called the Deez, Doze, Dems Guys.

They piled out singularly each one dressed in a gray union suit covered by bib overalls, and each of them wore high top, steel toe, black shoes and white socks. You would swear they were all brothers seemingly cloned from a Slavic organism. They were tall, fair complexioned, long sandy hair, and they all walked with the same stooped over-stride.

Methodically, like a line of busy ants, they removed everything from the bus and moved into Lakeview. All the while there was a continuous muted droning, *"Rumis sumoya dobromska,"* followed by, *"Coleski poplas pupulski rogoya,"* then, *"Wrisock dupasna."* What the hell all that ever meant none of us knew except perhaps Knobby. He would stand with this hands on his hips supervising their move.

"No more than five of you guys can sleep in that cabin," Knobby yelled.

"Rumis zumashka dobrowskis," they replied in unison.

"Yeah, I know, but there better not be more than five of you sleeping in that cabin."

Then it was either Paul or Vince or Walt or Peter (there was never an apparent leader of this group) who would say smartly, "Yaseer Veeknow."

"And park that bus between these two cabins. I want it out of sight."

"Yaseer Veeknow."

These commands would then be followed with continuous muted droning among the Skis.

One time when they tried to park the bus between the cabins it was like watching a Mack Sennett and the Keystone Cops movie. Paul seemed to be the most intelligent and he started maneuvering the bus around the pine trees. He motioned to Vince to guide him so that he could see his arm signals through the open passenger door. The other Skis stood around and watched.

"Whoa," yelled Vince whose arms indicated he wanted

Paul to angle left.

"Whoa," yelled Vince again as his arms this time showed Paul to steer right.

"*Wrisock dupasna,*" the others shouted.

Paul was also by now muttering, "*Duspa dumkas progoska.*"

"Whoa," yelled Vince, who by this time had helped Paul cozy the bus between two towering pines and on an angle that placed one side of the bus flush against the cabin.

"Get that bus away from the cabin," Knobby demanded.

Paul was now furious and waved his hands at Vince who checked the clearance behind the bus and showed Paul with his hands that it was about two feet from one of the pines. Paul put the bus in reverse and soundly smacked the pine tree. "*Dumka rumis,*" he yelled. And now the rest of the Skis were yelling and waving their arms giving Paul directions.

"Get ur ass in disboos now," Paul shouted.

Vince steadied himself with his left hand on the open doorway before he climbed aboard the bus. Paul was looking ahead at the others and grabbed the handle lever and shut the bus door. It closed on Vince's left hand.

"Whoa! *Rogoyavich sumkooska, Yigh! Yigh! Yigh!*" Vince screamed as he stumbled with the bus moving forward.

The other Skis roared, slapped each other on the back of their bib overalls, and did a little jig, "*Coleski poplas pupulski.*"

Paul opened the bus door after finally realizing he had closed it on Vince's hand. Vince squirmed on the ground. Knobby walked away shaking his head and containing a laugh. "What did I do to deserve this?" he asked himself.

The Polishers fished heavily and they brought in everything they caught—even the clams that somehow attached themselves to the hook. Their biggest delight was catching skinny northern pike.

"Those are hammer handles," Big Joe would say.

"Ya goot."

"Those are like eating snakes," Little Joe would add.
"Ya goot."

All the Polishers would pitch in doing the cooking. They chopped up those skinny northerns (after cleaning them in the sink) and used whatever else they brought in from the lake, then mixed all that with an assortment of vegetables, graced with garlic and hunks of their kielbasa. Polish fish stew they called it. The smell was enough that skunks moved out of the area.

They were not as dumb as they would appear as evidenced by the occasion when Big Joe pulled into the dock with a good stringer of walleyes. Four or five of the Polishers were standing on the dock muttering and droning their muted communications.

"Vair get dos?"

Big Joe was not about to divulge the spot he caught the fish so he said, "You know where Bear Paw point is by the crooked pine tree that leans out in the water?"

"Ya Veeknow."

"Well, fish about 50 yards out from that tree and you'll be right over a weed bed."

"Goot Veegonow."

Big Joe walked away with his catch smiling and saying to himself, "Those guys will fall for anything. Bear Paw my ass."

Later that day two boats pulled in and eight of the Skis jumped on shore muttering loudly, *"Rumis zumoya dobromska."* They had the nicest stringers of walleyes that had been caught in recent years here.

Big Joe was in the Lounge and heard about their catch. He hurried down to the dock. "My God! Where did you get those whoppers?"

"Veegoto Bear Paw."

"Bear Paw? You gotta be kidding."

"Notso. Veegit 100 yards out from datree."

"Well, I'll be damned." Big Joe said.

That night the Polishers ate well, drank a lot of their homemade wine, and danced a polka or two together. The foursome that adjourned to sleep in their bus laughed and one of them said, "Bear Paw his dupa."

Not all the same Skis came every year to fish Knobby's but any newcomer had a Ski in their ancestry somewhere. One year, to the delight of the entire camp, they brought with them a tall, blonde, statuesque woman. When she got off their bus Knobby caught his breath before yelling to them about where to park the bus. Knobby went up to Paul and asked, "What's with the gal?"

"She Vince's friend. She cook goot."

"Well, that's all she better do."

"Ya, she cook."

Her name was Sophie Bugleski and apparently she was a good cook because there was never a pungent odor when she made the northern pike-plus-other-stuff-stew.

Sophie was also an exercise fanatic and early every morning she would slink with long strides around the entire camp. When Moose Weinantz heard about this he was up at the crack of dawn hoping to meet her. He did.

"I'm really into walking in the morning," he said to Sophie who just kept slinking with her long strides. Eyes straight ahead. Moose had to trot to catch up with her. "It clears your head and fills your lungs with fresh air," he said. Sophie never wavered her stride. Eyes straight ahead. "Don't you think walking improves your lungs?" Moose asked.

No response from Sophie whose long blonde hair flowed from her pace. Moose had to run this time to catch up with her. He coughed then asked, "Don't you ever walk at night?"

This went on for over a mile and Moose was forever catching up with Sophie to pursue his one-man conversation. He finally quit and bent over panting and gasping for breath as she strode in to Lakeview cabin. That night Moose didn't show up at the Lounge.

"Where's Casanova Weinantz tonight?" someone asked.

"He's so pooped out and stiff from trying to walk this morning with the Polish broad," Big Joe said, "that he can't get out of bed."

Another newcomer showed up one year as the Polish Express pulled in. He was an older man, runty like, built like a linebacker, and contrary to the customary attire he wore the kind of pants and shirt like gasoline attendants wear. Knobby could soon tell he was not tracking with the others because he never muttered or droned, *"Rumis sumoya dombromska."* Whenever he said anything it was always, "Guddum Guddum Sumbich." He just stood around and stared at the activity saying, "Guddum." Whenever they wanted him to do something, they would show, point or lead him in the right direction. They called him Polack John and Knobby found out that he had been gassed in World War I.

Polack John did all their clean up work which Knobby appreciated. Every day he would carry their garbage can to the bait shack where he loaded it on the pick up truck Ralph took to the dump. Polack John was strong as an ox. Then he would carry an empty garbage can back to the cabin. Sam the Chummer took a liking to Polack John right away because he was in charge of their garbage.

"You find any plastic bottles give them to me," Sam told him one day. John just stared and replied, "Guddum Sumbich," but the next day John did find a plastic bottle in someone else's garbage and gave it to Sam. Sam shook his hand and Polack John smiled. "Guddum."

The two of them hung around together and Sam introduced Polack John to Ralph. John appeared fascinated at the way Ralph dipped out and counted minnows so fast. Polack John would put his hand in the swirling water of the minnow tank trying to grab one of the silvery fishes.

"Here, you gotta use this dip net," Ralph said.

Polack John lowered the dip net into the water then brought it up quickly. Minnows scattered all over. He dropped to his knees and tried to pick them up with his fingers. The minnows would slip through and Polack John would laugh and laugh. "Guddum Guddum Sumbich Guddum."

"That's enough dipping for awhile," Ralph said.

Polack John was also fascinated at the way Ralph operated the small riding mower. He followed Ralph around the camp as he mowed the grass and weeds along the shoreline and among the cabins. Ralph knew that Polack John wanted to run the mower so he always shook his head at John and said, "No. No. You can't run this thing." Even Knobby noticed Polack John tagging after Ralph. "I don't care if he helps you once in awhile," Knobby told Ralph, "but keep him away from that mower."

Early one morning the camp was awakened by the noise of the power motor scooting through the woods chewing up everything in its path. It was not Ralph who was up this early operating the mower, but Polack John who zig-zagged around trees and laughed loudly. Sam the Chummer tried to head him off, then Big Joe came out of the cabin shirtless and tried to catch John but it was meant to be. Polack John and the mower headed straight for the boat ramp area. Down the slight incline it chugged and into the water it slid. John continued to stay in the seat and laughed as the water engulfed the mower. "Guddum Sumbich Guddum."

In the days after, Ralph spent a lot of time repairing the mower with Polack John looking over this shoulder. "No! No!" Ralph said. Polack John smiled.

The reason the Polisher brought a lot of corrugated cartons was because they would fill them with large rocks they found in the shallow water. They loaded their boats with rocks, then packed the rocks in the cartons. Besides rocks they combed the shoreline for driftwood and by the time they were ready to leave camp the bus would be loaded down with all this collection. It was surprising that the springs of the bus held up from the weight. Knobby didn't mind their clearing the shoreline of driftwood but he did raise the bloody devil when he caught one of them walking away with a beautiful piece of driftwood that Knobby displayed in the front of his cabin. The Polishers sold the rocks and driftwood to some landscaping company and made enough to pay for their trip.

When the Polish Express departed its front end tilted skyward and Knobby was always glad to have them on their way. Except one year they left and forgot one of their passengers—Polack John. He must have been walking in the woods trying to track down Ralph but there he was all by himself and the Polish Express more than four hours on its way.

"What are we going to do with him?" Ralph asked Knobby.

"We ought to tie a bell around his neck," Knobby replied.

"No, really Knobby. What's going to happen with old John?"

"Well, how about you be in charge of him. You can have him help you with the garbage, minnows, generally clean up," Knobby said, "but no mower and don't get him boozed up."

Ralph thought that would work out and when Knobby said that Polack John could stay in the bunk house near the bait shack, Ralph felt even better. Polack John didn't seem to be aware of what was happening but continued to follow Ralph around and did a lot of general chores. "Guddum Guddum Sumbich." He slept in the bunk house and most of the people in camp saw that he had enough to eat.

One day he was not to be found and everyone was quite alarmed wondering what had happened to him. Jailer John was notified. A search party scoured the woods and the entire shoreline. Some wondered if the bears had gotten him or maybe he walked out into the water and drowned. The search went on for days and weeks and still no Polack John. Finally, all the camp regulars said they felt it was useless to continue looking for him. The belief was that he wandered into the woods, got lost, maybe fell, and that he met his unfortunate fate in the woods. Knobby had Jailer John contact the authorities in the city where the Polishers came from in hopes that someone might find the Ski who knew something about John. This was a sad time for people in camp but things did get back to normal soon enough.

The next year the Polish Express arrived on schedule in its yellow and red color scheme. The Skis filed out singularly in their union suits and bib overalls except for the last one who wore the pants and shirt of a gasoline station attendant. Polack John had returned to Knobby's. "Guddum Guddum."

14 | The Night They Tried to Put An End to 'Fisherman'

T. Randall Trinkle had more letters after his name than could be found in a can of alphabet soup. T. Randall Trinkle, B.A., A.M., L.L.B., J.D., Ph.D. He was a professor of humanities and philosophy at a small denominational college where he had established himself after acquiring all those degrees. He made no bones about wanting to be called Doctor but most of the gang at Knobby's acknowledged him as "Professor." He would say, "That's Doctor Trinkle, if you please." Ralph paid no attention whatsoever to the "Doctor" or "Professor" monikers and merely called him "TR" because he had heard Trinkle's wife call him that once.

Doctor Trinkle was of good size, about a 50 waist. His pants always hung a couple of inches above his ankles. He was bald but grey bearded and wore square granny glasses that were draped around his neck by a black elastic strap when they weren't perched on his stubby red nose. He constantly squinted through a pasty, fleshy face. One thing about Doctor Trinkle was that he always smelled like an old book. Always.

There was a slight trace of German accent but not enough to detract from his letter perfect elocution. When the Doctor spoke you were caught up in his oration.

His wife, Pauline, could have passed for his sister. Exactly the same body form and complexion but she had a full crop of orange hair and only a slight hint of facial hair under her nose.

They would stay at Knobby's for two full months in Tuckaway cabin where they literally holed up hardly going outside for days. Doctor Trinkle wrote things: papers, essays, letters, articles, items. Apparently some of his stuff was published nationally like his essays on: The Psychological Aftershocks of Earthquakes, A Moralist Views of A Loosey-Goosey Society, Trees, An Asset Beyond Joyce Kilmer's Fondest Dreams, and others of this genre.

Pauline spent all her waking hours lettering on round wooden plaques that still had the bark on them. The kind of wording she lettered were like: "He Who Obtains Has Little — He Who Scatters Has Much," "The Indian Scalps His Enemies — The White Man Skins His Friends," "Life Is Too Short to Be Little," "The Gift Without The Giver Is Bare," and other cliche sayings. She would paint pretty flowers, bells, sprigs, decorations kinds of things along the edges of the sayings.

Actually her plaques were quite nice and she gave some of them to various people who were in camp. She gave one to Marge McFarland that read, "You Have Not Converted A Woman Because You Have Silenced Her." Mac wouldn't let Marge hang it in their cabin. But Knobby had the plaque she gave him right near the fireplace in the Lounge. It read, "He

Who Cuts His Own Wood Is Twice Warmed."

The other plaques she took back with her and sold them to some gift shop in their small college town. But can you imagine both of them holed up all day in their cabin for two months not saying hardly a word to each other. He contemplating and writing. She lettering and painting. And both of them smelling like old books.

The Doctor called it their summer sabbatical where they could get away and reflect on life and absorb the serenity of God's world. Early every morning this serenity ritual was broken when Doctor Trinkle would go out on their porch, pound his round chest with his fists and loudly state, "Oh it's another great day." The Happy Hour gang stayed in a nearby cabin and they never took kindly to this early awakening, and KJ would reply even louder from inside their cabin, "That's a matter of opinion."

The Happy Hour gang got even with Doctor Trinkle one night. They had a large ham bone they were going to put in the outside garbage can but instead KJ placed it on the front step of Trinkle's cabin. He knew the skunks making their nightly rounds would find it and hopefully leave behind some of their smothering scent. What KJ hadn't planned on was even better. Bruno, the camp's big black Labrador, found the ham bone first and proceeded to gnaw away on it in front of Trinkle's cabin. Two skunks came upon Bruno and all hell broke loose. He wouldn't release the bone, but they released a lot of fumes that smarted your eyes if you got close.

The barking got louder, the smell stronger, and Doctor Trinkle got up to see what was occurring. As soon as he went outside on the screened porch, the odor hit him full blast. He orated loudly and distinctly, "That is the rankest smell that ever has offended my nostrils," and rushed inside.

Doctor Trinkle and Pauline were very undisturbed mostly about everything. They never fished so whenever anyone

brought in a good catch they never "Oh'd" or "Ah'd" like the others. They just were oblivious to matters that went on around them like the time the bear came to their cabin. The big black bear sniffed some food on their porch, smashed through the screen door, broke open the cooler and chomped on the fruit and vegetables. Pauline got up and looked on the porch and saw the rounded back of the bear. She merely said, "If that's you, TR, you can let yourself in. The door's unlocked." Doctor Trinkle was asleep in the other bedroom.

There was only one time when the Trinkles stirred the waters enough that Knobby and some others were ready to escort them personally on their way back to the small college town. The Trinkles almost created a statewide controversy. No, it would have been a nationwide controversy.

You see, Knobby was smarter than a lot of people gave him credit for. He decided some time ago to have an informal committee made up of camp regulars who would meet every couple of weeks to discuss any problems or improvements that he should be concerned about. The committee would then take the heat off him if they decided to take some specific action. It was a great idea because hardly anything ever got discussed because things got taken care of without a lot of formality anyway.

The Grounds Committee, as they called themselves, consisted of Mac McFarland, Pops Robertson, Big Joe, Sam the Chummer, and Knobby. They would meet on a Tuesday night in the Lounge and end up playing cards and drinking beer. Except for one night.

Doctor Trinkle saw Knobby and asked, "My spouse and I, and some of our acquaintances would like to join you at your session tonight."

"What's on your mind?"

"We have an item that needs clarification. Is 7:30 acceptable?"

"Yeah, I guess so but maybe we can clear up the matter right now."

"Hardly. This has been a point of contention with me for years and requires great deliberation."

When the Ground Committee assembled that night it was as lethargical as usual. They were all seated around one of the tables. Big Joe was working a crossword puzzle and Pops was helping him. Mac glanced through a fishing magazine, and Sam just sat there upset because Pops was helping with the crossword and not he. Ralph was tending bar so Knobby could handle committee matters. Only a few others were in the Lounge.

"We're gonna have company tonight, fellows," Knobby said. "The Professor and some of his friends want to talk about something."

"What's on his mind?" asked Mac.

"Beats the hell out of me," Knobby said. Then in came a parade led by the Trinkles and Henrietta Schwartzhopf. The three of them looked like a tent convention. They were followed by Marge McFarland, DeeDee Duval, and her two girlfriends. They all pulled up some chairs and circled the table. Moose Weinantz and some others seated at the bar moved over to the arena.

Doctor Trinkle stood up. "Gentlemen, we want to place a motion before the committee," he said and opened a folder and began reading, "In the interests of promulgating equal identification and fostering consistent and appropriate communication, yet with utmost appreciation, sensitivity, and genuine regard for what has been traditional behavior and acceptance, we hereby submit the following motion:

"When a female fishes individually she shall be called Fisherwoman. When fishing with members of the same sex they shall be referred to as Fisherwomen. When a female fishes with a member of the opposite sex they shall be referred to as Fisherpeople or Fisherpersons.

"The conditions set forth in this motion shall take effect immediately in any written and oral communications."

Knobby was dumbstruck. Up sprung Marge. "I second that."

"For Crisake, Marge. Sit down," shouted Mac.

"Let me see if I understand what you're trying to say." said Knobby.

"Veer not traying toosay. Veer sayink it," replied Henrietta.

Mac interrupted, "You're saying you want to be called 'Fisherwoman' or 'Fisherperson'?"

"You've got it!"

"Sit down, Marge, for Crisake," said Mac. "You've gotta

be kidding. This doesn't make any sense at all."

"You been sniffing something in your cabin, Professor?" asked Knobby.

"Let's hear what they got to say," yelled Moose moving closer to the two girlfriends.

Now Pauline stood up and articulated, "We go hunting and we are called Hunters. We use a bow and arrow and are referred to as Archers. We camp and are called Campers. And on it goes like this," she continued. "Trappers, Shooters, Backpackers, Boaters. We don't have any quarrel with this type of nomenclature, but put us in a boat or on a bank with a rod and reel and we end up being called Fishermen. And we're getting tired of it."

The activists applauded.

DeeDee then stood up, coughed, cleared her throat, took a deep drag from her cigarette and spoke about all the women bowlers, golfers, swimmers who are never called Bowlermen, Golfermen, or Swimmermen.

More loud applause from the activists.

Moose jumped up and unfortunately said, "I suppose you want to call us something else too!"

"We were thinking about Pikers!" DeeDee answered quickly.

Knobby and the Grounds Committee were losing control of the meeting. "You realize, of course, you're asking to change something that's been in place for a heckuva long time," Knobby said. "If we ever started doing what you're proposing, we'd be the laughing stock of the whole state, the whole country," he added.

Big Joe handed his crossword puzzle to Pops, stood up and said, "I may have the solution. How about settling for the word Angler. Izaak Walton wouldn't object."

Marge responded, "Well, you don't seem to call your-selves that, and besides Angler sounds a little contriving. How would you feel about saying we were angling last weekend and caught a mess?"

Mac couldn't restrain himself. "Marge, you're right. You never caught a mess in your life. Now, for Crisake, sit down."

Big Joe had the floor again and said, "Angling is no more misleading than saying we were fishing around."

Then one of DeeDee's girlfriends spoke up, "That's a lot better than hearing you men talk about going out trolling."

Moose Weinantz moved his chair even closer to her.

Once again Big Joe got their attention and said with all the dignity he could muster, "I believe I may finally have the solution. Why don't you call yourselves Fishwives?"

Then things really got out of hand.

"Some of us aren't married," said DeeDee.

"Yeah, she's right ya big clown," said the other girlfriend. Moose moved his chair away.

Ralph wandered over from the bar knowing things were getting out of hand. "Would anyone care for some liquid refreshment?"

"Yeah," replied the Grounds Committee.

"Not now," yelled the activists.

Knobby tried to wiggle out of the predicament and said, "It's been a long night and we hear what you're trying to say." He cleared his throat. "I suggest we appoint a committee and have them present something next month. Whattya say?"

He knew most of them would be gone by then and his suggestion received an overwhelming, "NO."

Sam the Chummer was one person who had not spoken out all night. He stood up slowly to address the group. One of DeeDee's girlfriends snickered.

"Ladies and Gentlemen," he said squeakily. "What the hell! I've been sittin' here for some time now and I ain't heard hardly anything. But it's the most excitement I've seen around here in ages."

Sam continued, "Big Joe's had some good ideas but he and Pops are stuck on solving 25 Across. And poor Ralph. He ain't had any business all night and that's bad." Sam was quiet for a moment then said, "What can be good is if all of us can leave here tonight still as friends because we thrashed through something."

It was startling how quiet the entire Lounge was as old Sam continued, "I recall Izaak Walton writing, 'I love such mirth as does not make friends ashamed to look upon one another next morning.' "

Doctor Trinkle sat with his mouth open. Pauline smiled. Marge looked over at Mac and winked. Henrietta nudged DeeDee so hard she almost fell to the floor.

Sam was still on his feet. He put out both arms like a preacher. "If you all don't mind let me offer a suggestion. What the hell. How about calling everyone Piscators? Now I've got to get to the bathroom before I float."

15 Gus, the Game Warden

The first official game warden to cover the Lake of Six Rivers area was James MacLeod. But he was more than a game warden to people at Knobby's. Congenial to everyone he was a confidant to many. On several occasions he actually went out of his way to help people fish. Once when Pops Robertson came in empty handed, which didn't happen often, MacLeod said to him, "Have you tried using crickets yet this year? I heard the 'gills were going after crickets at Stone Lake last week. You might try 'em."

Pops thanked MacLeod and the next day caught a mess of bluegills on crickets. He told Knobby, "You tell MacLeod he gets a haircut anytime he wants."

Whenever MacLeod was standing around the dock and saw someone come in skunked, he would tell them where he thought they might catch some bass or perch. And most of the time he was right.

Warden MacLeod never bothered anyone at Knobby's. He went by the philosophy that anyone who loves to fish and is devoted to the sport knows the rules and plays by the rules. Besides he had an uncanny way of suspecting if any wrong was underfoot. All he had to do was look the person directly in their eyes and MacLeod could tell if they were on the up and up. He always asked Moose Weinantz to remove his sunglasses when Moose talked to him.

Some people in this part of the country, however, thought he was tough and cranky because he made his share of arrests at some of the other more commercial fishing spots. But not at Knobby's. Warden MacLeod was more like a welcomed visitor who always shared whatever news he had and listened to whatever complaints people wanted to get off their minds, then he acted on them.

He and Knobby were fairly close since they were about the same age, same type of background, and MacLeod worked on the garbage trucks years ago with Knobby. Whenever Warden MacLeod got ready to leave after his visit he always had a chat with Knobby in the Lounge and his usual shot of whiskey.

"Knobby, I think I'm going to get transferred to headquarters," he said fingering his shot glass.

"Well, you're moving up in the world, MacLeod," said Knobby. "You deserve a promotion."

"Don't think I'm going to like the desk job as much as I like being out in the open."

"You'll get used to it," Knobby replied. "What they going to have you do?"

"Guess I'm going to be in charge of all the game wardens in the district. How does that sound?" MacLeod downed his whiskey.

"Well, I'm glad for you. You've worked hard," Knobby said patting MacLeod on the back. "That calls for another shot."

"No thanks, Knob', but you may need one after I tell you who my replacement is."

Knobby waited.

"Looks like August Severson's going to take over my territory," MacLeod said.

"Don't think I know him."

"You soon will, He's Lars Severson's nephew and has a reputation of being just like old Lars."

"Oh, that's just great! Can't you put someone else in the job now that you're in charge?" asked Knobby.

"Not right now. Gus is next in line for this territory and until he screws up I can't do anything about it."

It had been a long time since Knobby had any dealings with the Seversons. Old Lars stubbed his toe on a big real estate venture some years ago when he bought up acres and acres of timber land after being told a large paper corporation was eyeing up the property. Lars used all his assets for collateral but the deal fell through since the paper corporation went out of state for their timber. The blow left Lars penniless and mentally incapacitated. He now was living in obscurity in a nursing home. Jailer John had leaked out this bit of information since his job was to know what was going on in town.

August Severson turned out to be just what MacLeod had predicted. He became a royal pain in the butt. His first entrance to Knobby's had him almost leaping from the brown state-owned car. He was spit and polish, very stiff, official looking. He just happened to hit the siren button enough to have it start momentarily with that deep throated *EEEeeeR-RRrrr*. Although short it was loud enough to get people's attention.

"I'm August Severson, the new game warden for these parts," he pompously announced to Knobby and the others in the Lounge. "I'll be checking on things around here and will expect your cooperation."

"We always cooperate," Knobby replied.

"Good. Let's start by looking at your fishing license receipts for the year."

It was the first time Knobby had to open these books to anyone but Gus the Game Warden went over every name on the register, and added up all the money received from the licenses. Knobby tightened but stood patiently.

"Do you have the documentation for the money you sent the state for these licenses?" Gus asked.

"It's around here somewhere," Knobby said, "If you get out of the way maybe I can find it."

Knobby rummaged through some papers in the drawer while Gus the Game Warden arrogantly strolled around the Lounge looking at all the mounted fish on the walls.

"Hmm, a striped bass, eh?"

Knobby continued searching through the accumulation of papers paying no attention or commenting to the inspection Gus was giving to the stuffed fish.

"I presume all these fish were caught properly and in season," Gus commented.

Finally, Knobby found the paper, showed it to Gus, got a terse nod of approval, and Gus sauntered out and strolled to the dock. He glanced officially over the boat ramp, beach, water, back across the cabins, then strutted back to the brown car. It's tires tossed out small stones as Gus the Game Warden wheeled the car around the driveway and sped out the narrow lane.

"I hope that's the last we see of that horse's ass," Knobby said watching the cloud of dust proceeding through the trees.

"I'll drink to that," replied Ralph.

It was by no means the last of Gus the Game Warden's visits to Knobby's. At first it was almost daily inspections then he tapered to at least weekly intrusions. All very official and authoritative but a real pain in the butt.

Gus the Game Warden checked everything. He took down the boat registration numbers and compared them to Knobby's records and against the state records. He checked the bait house to see if there were any illegal minnows or improper bait being made available.

Ralph came storming into the Lounge one afternoon shouting, "Get that SOB outta here or I'm going to drown him in one of the tanks."

Gus the Game Warden waited stoically and magisterially by the water's edge for incoming boats. He asked everyone to show him the fish they caught so he could personally measure each fish for its legal length. He counted every fish. He asked people for their licenses. It wasn't that Gus the Game Warden was out of line doing what he did. It was the manner in which he conducted his investigation that honked people off.

"That smart alec had nerve enough to ask me if I knew all the fishing regulations," McFarland yelled at Knobby. "For Crisake, Marge. I thought you knew all the answers."

Gus almost nailed the Polishers about the size of their fish but when he saw all the skinny northerns he thought better of it. "You people eat these things?" he asked. *"Rumis sumoya dobromska,"* followed by *"Coleski poplas pupulski rogoya."* Gus knew he wouldn't get anywhere or make any authoritative impression with the Polishers.

"I better not find you people stepping on the fish. You here?" And he marched off seeking some other supposed offender. One of the Polishers laughed, *"Butzowy myne dupa."*

This kind of harassment went on for weeks at a time and those in camp were even starting to get at each other's throats. Gus the Game Warden threatened Sam about littering the water with his plastic bottles. Then he got on Big Joe for visually polluting the place with his signs. He accused Fibber Farquahar of lying. He almost wrote up Zucky for operating an unsafe boat. All this was ending up in Knobby's lap because these guests were starting to demand that he do something to quell this type of indecency.

"I say we hang him by his toes," said Ralph.

"I say we feed him to the bears," said Moose.

Knobby went to town and called his friend MacLeod and told him what was happening. MacLeod, however, said that his hands were tied because what Gus was doing was all on the up and up and he couldn't reprimand him for doing something that was technically part of his job. "How about style?" Knobby said. "It stinks."

"I need proof that he's acting out of authority, is destroying people's property, is morally damaging the department," MacLeod stated. "Right now, Knob' old friend, there's not a lot I can do."

Unfortunately, MacLeod was right and Gus the Game Warden continued obnoxiously exercising his duties in this pompous manner. Late one night he even waited by the shore for the Italian Connection to come in from fishing. Gus didn't realize he could be taking his life in his own hands by trying to accost this group in the dark. When they pulled in Gus lit up the area with his multi-cell flashlight. Vinnie and Carmie scampered out and ran for Breezy Point. Tony and Vito stood up trying to shield their eyes from the light.

"Been fishing, eh?"

"Yeah, what's it to ya," replied Vito.

"Nothing except I'm August Severson, the game warden for these parts and I want to see your licenses."

"We weren't fishing," said Tony.

"Just a nighttime cruise," added Vito.

Gus smiled drolly. "Then why all the poles?"

"That's for practicing in case we ever do want to fish," said Tony. By now Vinnie and Carmie had reappeared and were standing behind Gus.

"Do you or do you not have licenses?"

"We don't have licenses 'cause we don't fish," said Vito.

"We all got lifetime passes for this place," Tony added.

"Well, you've told me what I suspected. You said you

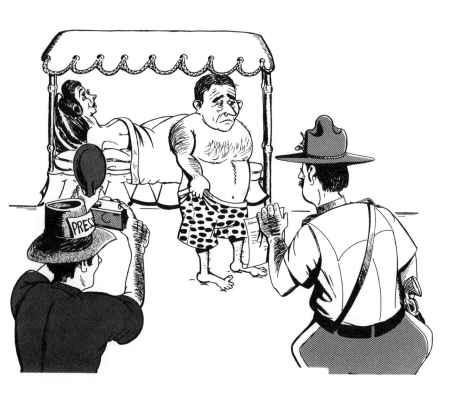

were fishing then you said you don't have licenses," Gus stated and took a pad from his chest pocket. Vinnie and Carmie reached inside their jackets.

"I'm writing you all up and fining you for fishing without a license."

The four of them laughed but Gus stood ground, wrote out the ticket, and handed it to Vito. "See you in court," he said and strutted off to the brown car.

"Somma bitch! Carmie, go get Knobby and tell him we want to see him," said Vito. "Now."

They told Knobby what had happened and Knobby gave the Italian Connection the full story about Gus the Game Warden and what he was doing to the camp. When Knobby left Breezy Point Tony said, "Your worries are over Knobby."

You would have thought the newspaper in town would have toned down the story that appeared a few weeks following the Italian Connection's conversation with Knobby. The two-column headline read: "GAME WARDEN NABBED IN SEX RAID."

Somehow or other August Severson, a family man, diligent provider, law upholding state employee was found with one of the ladies of pleasure in her room at a house of ill repute. It just so happened that Jailer John was alerted to the occasion and a newspaper reporter showed up at the scene of the fleshy tryst at the same time. Gus the Game Warden literally leaped from the bed as the blinding flashbulbs went off. Jailer John laughed as he read the words about Gus having rights.

James MacLeod had no other choice but to discharge Gus from his duties as game warden and assign him elsewhere in a capacity involving Smokey the Bear signs. MacLeod dropped by Knobby's shortly after. He walked around the area. Smiled at those nearby and waved to others. He joined Knobby in the Lounge.

"Knob', looks like you got the job done. I'll have that other shot now."

16 | The Hoot And Holler Fishing Tournament

At one of the sessions of the so-called Grounds Committee Knobby quite casually made a comment, "Maybe some year we ought to hold a fishing tournament." The words apparently fell on deaf ears. But if it wasn't for Sam the Chummer's inability to hear well, the tournament may never have gotten off the ground.

The next day wherever Knobby made his rounds the questions were always the same. "When you gonna hold the tournament?", "Have you set the rules for the tournament?", "Count us in, Knobby."

Sam had done such an excellent job of communicating the possibilities of a fishing tournament that people were led to believe it was definitely going to happen and all they needed was to know when.

"Thanks, Sam for telling everybody about the tournament," Knobby said sarcastically. "We ought to put you in charge."

"What the hell!" Sam replied.

The Grounds Committee reassembled for one of their rare unscheduled meetings and discussed the tournament, and all agreed it was a good idea. Sam even tried to make a motion to that effect. "Sit down," said Big Joe. "You already contributed enough on this thing."

Pops said he thought it was a good idea to hold it towards the end of summer as kind of a bonus to all the regulars who fished here during the year.

And Mac agreed saying, "The end of August is a slow time, Knobby. Maybe this would bring in more business."

"Let's call it Knobby's Annual Hoot and Holler Fishing Tournament," exclaimed Big Joe.

"Hoot and Holler?" asked Mac. "Why Hoot and Holler?"

"Because when anyone catches fish around here they always make some kind of noise like hooting or hollering," said Big Joe.

"Well, I don't," Mac commented.

"No, you don't," added Pops. "You just say, 'For Crisake, Marge, sit down'."

"Don't either."

"I just say 'hot diggity damn'," said Sam.

"Well, I don't have any opinion about calling it 'Hoot and Holler' but we ain't gonna call it 'Annual'," Knobby said.

On and on the conversation went like this and the Grounds Committee wasn't getting anywhere in firming up the tournament until Big Joe said, "Let's resolve this. Everyone agree to a tournament?"

Everyone agreed.

"Okay. Pops, Mac and I will write up the rules," said Big Joe. "Okay?"

Everyone agreed except Sam. "What the hell! What's the matter with me?"

"You can edit the rules after we have them," Big Joe replied.

Knobby raised the question, "How does a Sunday sound? Like August 14?"

Everyone agreed and adjourned the most productive meeting thus far held by the Grounds Committee. "We've got a lot of work ahead of us, men," said Big Joe. "About three weeks to pull this thing off."

Knobby shook his head wondering about the wisdom of his chance suggestion. But in a few days Big Joe had everyone assembled again for a review of the rules and regulations they had prepared. In the meantime the camp was already aware that Sunday, August 14 Knobby's First Annual Hoot and Holler Fishing Tournament would be held. Sam had struck again. There was now a sense of excitement in the hot summer air.

"Are you ready for the rules?" Big Joe said standing among the committee. "Here they are:

"1. No more than two persons per boat and no more than two poles per person."

"That will eliminate the Polishers," laughed Sam.

"Be quiet and listen to the rules," Big Joe said and continued.

"2. The boat that catches the most fish will be declared the grand prize winner.

"3. The boat that catches the biggest fish will get a special award."

"What's that?" asked Sam.

"We'll tell you later," said Mac.

"4. If two or more boats tie for quantity, the winner will be the one that has the biggest fish. The biggest fish will be determined by weight not length. If two fish weigh the same, then length will determine the winner."

"Geez, that sounds hard to figure out," said Sam. "What the hell, we could be all night judging this thing."

"Be quiet and just listen," Big Joe said.

"Well, you said I was to edit the rules," Sam replied.

"5. It shall be unlawful for any boat to tie-up or drop anchor to fish within 50 feet of another boat that is already fishing if it in any way disturbs that boat's lines."

Knobby shook his head perplexed.

"6. Any boat caught cheating in any manner will be disqualified.

"7. Fish species eligible for the tournament will be: suckers, carp, perch, walleyes, northern pike, largemouth and smallmouth bass, bluegills, molly-hogs, catfish, sunfish, rock bass, hickory shad, white perch, and crappies."

"Now, men did I leave out any other kind?"

"Yeah," said Sam. "How about striped bass?"

Big Joe made a face like he was in pain and continued.

"8. Turtles, shinners, dogfish, gar, knotheads will not be eligible."

"You better make sure the Polishers understand that," said Sam.

"Be quiet and listen."

"9. All eligible fish caught must be at least their legal length.

"10. It shall be unlawful to use droplines, trotlines, gigs, cross bows, snares, gill nets, traps, clubs or other devices of this nature.

"11. The tournament will start at 9:00 AM. and conclude at 2:00 PM. Any boat returning to the judging area after 2:00 PM will be disqualified.

"12. There will be a $5.00 entry fee for each boat with the grand prize winner receiving all this money."

"I'll take care of the beer, brats, hamburgers, the whole

spread afterwards," Knobby proclaimed.

"That's nice of you, Knobby," they replied.

"What about the biggest fish?" Sam asked.

"We're getting to that," said Big Joe. "Mac, you want to tell him?"

Mac said he would like to. "Sam, since you got most of the big fish hanging here in this Lounge, we thought you'd like to handle having the biggest fish caught mounted and placed permanently here in the Lounge."

Sam thought about it for awhile then said, "Yeah, what the hell. That's okay I'll probably get the biggest anyway."

The others didn't comment since they got Sam to agree to taking care of the biggest fish award.

It didn't take long for Big Joe to write up the rules and print out the notice which was posted in the Lounge. It didn't take Sam long either to get the word out and stimulate interest in the tournament. After the first week eight boats had signed up and deposited their entry fee. The McFarlands, Big Joe and Plumb Joe sponsored by Dunn's Plumbing, Little Joe and Moose Weinantz with Moose working hard for a sponsor to cough up the entry fee, Tonto Tom and Fibber Farquahar sponsored by O'Brien's Chevy, Paul Laskowski and Walt Malinski, Pops, Sam who wouldn't double up with anyone since he didn't want them to know his secrets, and the surprise entry was Jailer John and DeeDee Duval sponsored by DeeDee's Pies.

Then some others in camp entered, and a few more from town heard about it and they signed up making the total fourteen boats for the tournament. You should have seen the preparations in the days before Sunday, like ants attacking a sweet morsel. Tonto Tom hauled in a real honest-to-goodness fishing boat with a 20 horse motor. Then the arguing started in.

"I thought we said no motors over 15 horsepower," said

Mac.

"We didn't say anything about motors," commented Big Joe.

"What the hell! They'll be churning up the whole lake," added Sam.

"All the Fibber said was that he would be fishing with Tonto," Big Joe replied.

"Hell, he lies all the time," Sam said.

Then later Sam got caught coming in with several empty buckets of worms he had used to chum one of his special holes. The Polishers nailed him on this one and went directly to Knobby.

"Why he trow dos wurms in water?"

"He wanted to get rid of some he had," said Knobby.

"No vair. He cheat. Vesee him by Bear Paw trowing wurms in water. Dat our place."

Knobby tried to explain that nobody had rights to any place and that they could fish wherever they like. The Polishers weren't happy with his resolution and stalked off with their usual *"Rumis wrisock dupasna."*

Sam pulled another slick trick when he went out on another night and placed all the white plastic bottles he had deposited all around the lake in places where dynamite wouldn't raise a fish. Then he dropped green colored plastic bottles over his favorite spots hoping the contestants would look for the white markers.

The Grounds Committee waited until the last minute to decide who the judges would be and that caused another ruckus. Pops kiddingly suggested Professor Trinkle and his wife Pauline.

"Not on your cotton-picking life."

"No way."

"You gotta be out of your mind."

"You must be smelling too much hair tonic."

"I think he's drinking the stuff."

"I hope you're not serious."

"The tournament's called off," said Knobby.

But they finally agreed on what was a logical choice and the participants wouldn't argue with the decision. Tony Tufano and Vito Giovannetti were in camp and they wouldn't be fishing during the day, especially on a Sunday, and they would be impartial and forceful judges. Knobby asked them and they were pleased to have the opportunity.

Sunday morning, August 14 was bright and steamy warm. All the participants were moving about like a fart on a griddle. Knobby tried loudly to cover the general rules again but most of them were more interested in socializing and giving each other some good natured kidding about who was going to win.

"Ralph here is going to shoot off the gun to start the tournament. Then he's going to shoot it again at two o'clock in the afternoon when the tournament's over," Knobby yelled out. "All boats better be back here by two."

Moments later Ralph let out a blast from the old muzzle loader black powder gun. Fourteen boats rev'd up, banged against each other, whipped up the water, and looked like the great Oklahoma land rush was happening again only in water. Away they went to their favorite fishing spots far less amicable with each other than they had been.

"Get the hell outta our way," Moose yelled at the Polishers who were heading full speed for Bear Paw.

"Buttzowy myne dupa."

Big Joe and Plumb Joe were having trouble getting their barge-like boat heading in the right direction because of the wakes created by the others.

"Marge, for Crisake, start fishing."

"We aren't 100 yards from shore."

"Well, start anyway."

Jailer John steered their boat for a secluded bay he had staked out a week ago more for the seclusion than the fishing. DeeDee sat in front coughing and puffing on her cigarette.

Sam carefully avoided the earlier collisions and was already nearing some of his green plastic bottles.

Tonto Tom and the Fibber roared past him and over the plastic bottles with their prop cutting the anchor cords freeing all the bottles.

"What the hell!" Sam yelled. "You think you own the lake?"

Soon things quieted except for an occasional "Yahoo! I got one." Tonto and Fibber zoomed their boat all over the water and pulled up close to the two Joes.

"You're too close," yelled Big Joe standing up in their

boat.

"Getting anything?"

"We're fishing here. Now get the hell gone," Big Joe shouted.

Tonto and Fibber trolled around the Joe's boat closer than the rules stated.

"I'll show them," Big Joe muttered and whipped out his lure. It snagged the minnow bucket trailing from the other boat. Big Joe pulled hard and Tonto saw that he was hooked good. He started the motor and moved out into open water.

"Hey! I'm hooked up on your bucket," yelled Big Joe who had a death grip on his rod. Their barge-like boat was being pulled along stretching the ten pound test line to its maximum. When it snapped Big Joe tumbled backwards over the boat seat.

"You're disqualified," he yelled shaking his fist at the fast departing boat.

Sam kept moving from one green plastic bottle to another and hadn't caught a thing.

Pops was anchored against one of the dead trees that marked one of his quiet spots.

Moose kept insisting that Little Joe look for Jailer and DeeDee but Little Joe knew there would be few fish caught by these two.

Mac for once was almost whispering to Marge. "Thatta gal. Keep it up. We've got a good mess here."

Before two o'clock rolled around the intense competition had already brought the contestants back to shore for the judging. Ralph shot off the muzzle loader and Knobby yelled, "The tournament is officially over."

"Where's Tonto and Fibber?" someone asked.

"I hope they drowned," said Big Joe.

Actually, there was little judging to be done because Tony and Vito could easily see that McFarland's boat had the most fish. The Polishers tried to argue that they had more but some of their fish was indistinguishable.

"*Rumis sumoya.*"

"Shut your mouth," Vito snapped. "We're the judges for this here contest and we know what boat's got the most fish."

Tony handed the envelope containing the prize money to Mac, shook Mac's hand and said, "The grand prize winner of the First Annual Fishing Tournament at Knobby's is Mac Mc-Farland."

The others clapped their hands, whistled, hooted and hollered. Mac smiled and basked in this short lived attention.

"Just a minute, Homer Amos," Marge interrupted. "I caught all the fish so I get to keep the money." Marge grabbed the envelope from Mac and held it up in the air. The hooting and hollering was even louder.

"And the prize for the biggest fish goes to the Ski's," proclaimed Tony. "One of them, Paul or Walt, caught a five pound sucker."

More hooting and hollering. More "*Rumis sumoya.*"

Tony held up the five pound sucker for all to see then took it over to Sam. "I hear you're gonna get this mounted for these guys as their prize." He handed the fish to Sam but quick as a wink Paul Laskowski grabbed it. "Dis our fish," he said.

Knobby tried to intercede telling him that Sam was going to get it stuffed and it would go on the wall so others could see it. Walt Malinski stepped up and said, "Dis our fish. We keep."

Knobby shook his head. "Big Joe! Where are you?" he asked. "Maybe you can explain this to them." Knobby then went over to the tables where the refreshments were laid out. Big Joe couldn't get through to the Polishers either. Paul Laskowski held up the five pound sucker. "We keep. We eat," he said with a wide smile.

More hooting and hollering.

Sam looked relieved since he didn't have to get the damn thing mounted.

"The keg's open and the food's ready," yelled Knobby. "Let's dig in."

The rest of the afternoon was one of the biggest social events of the year. Any bruised egos from what could be considered a Les Mans start on water and other incidents soon simmered down. Pops was leading a group in three-part harmony. All the Polishers showed up for the spread and as soon as they filled their bellies, they put on a show of their ethnic dances. DeeDee coughed louder and the Jailer slapped her soundly on the back thinking she might be choking. She sputtered, "You trying to kill me?" Moose quickly went to her rescue. Mac told Traveling Salesman jokes. It was one fine party.

As the sun dipped behind the towering pines its rays cast out a panorama of expanding colors high up into the sky. Knobby looked up and suddenly started waving his arms. "Hey! Hey! Hold it everybody," he yelled. The crowd quieted slightly. "You know what today is?" Absolutely no response. "It's V-J Day!" Then Ralph got out the muzzle loader and boomed out a shot that reverberated through the woods. The hooting and hollering now was infectious. Mac kissed Marge. The Polishers kissed each other. Even the Jailer gave DeeDee a peck on her cheek.

Later in the evening when things were back more to an even keel, Tonto and the Fibber rowed their boat up to shore. They stepped out and walked up to the festivities. "Our motor conked out," Tonto said. "We think someone put sugar in the gas tank."

"Yeah," the Fibber added, "and I had just hooked into a twenty pound northern."

17 | Aches and Pains

Somehow serious accidents or afflictions seldom found their way or stayed around too long at Knobby's Place. Oh, sure there were the typical hooks imbedded in fingers, cuts, scrapes, scratches, sunburns, poison ivy, insect bites, and other assorted maladies but they ran their course and the recipients managed to fish again. About the most common malaise was the proverbial hangover. Many of those afflicted with this morning after tormentor adamantly claimed it was instead the flu bug that was aggravating their body from brains to bowels.

Henrietta Schwartzkopf conking herself on her chin with the butt of her fishing rod was probably the most serious of the accidents and fortunately that was more of a calamity than a catastrophe.

It was amazing that with all the horseplay and shenanigans going on here no one really got hurt, except for perhaps some pain to the personality. It wasn't those mischievous acts that began to take their toll. It was old age that started to make its inroads.

The morning calm was becoming penetrated by distressful sounds of "Ohs" and "Aws" as many of the regulars climbed into and out of their boats. Pops always tried to bend over and touch his knees before he got into his boat as he said, "in order to limber up."

Little Joe had arthritic knees from his football days and the humidity would play hell with him. Once he got in his boat he was there for a long time because getting out was just as painful. It was the same with Big Joe. Although his legs were in good shape, years of sign painting had cripped his fingers and he couldn't whip out his fishing rod as often and as fast as he once did. On the other hand, he was a little more comfortable because he could sit down in the boat ever since he had his hemorrhoids taken care of.

The aging process also affected Mac. He looked like a circus act getting in to his captain's-type chair. Once managing this he didn't move about as frisky as he once did. And Marge's pee can became much more in vogue. Most boats now carried a three pound coffee can as standard equipment.

Conversation typically once centered on lingo like:
"Citchanenny?"
"Goddafew."
"Kindarthay?"
"Bassencarp."
"Ennysizetoom?"
"Cuplapowns."
"Hittinhard?"
"Sordalike."
"Wahchoozin?"
"Gobbawurms."
"Seeyaroun."
"Yeahtakideezy."

In recent years the amenities among anglers were more along the lines of:
"Did you get your walk in this morning?"

"Went two miles down the road."

"How do you feel?"

"I'm able to be out."

"Have you had your morning constitution?"

"I'm pretty regular after using bran flakes."

"You're looking good."

"Thanks, but I feel like hell."

"Going fishing today?"

"Not unless it warms up."

Even the Happy Hour bunch went on a different time schedule in later years. Instead of returning to their cabin at 5:00 PM, they now headed back an hour earlier. KJ used to say, "I hope we don't miss happy hour," but mostly groaned, "My ass is cold and wet and I'm going to sit it on the stove."

Moose Weinantz had back problems and complained all the time. When he went out in the morning it was always, "Oh! My aching back." And when he returned it was, "Oh! My aching butt."

One of the Polishers fell out of their boat once and the only encouragement the rest of them gave him was, "Get ur ass in disboat now." It was the same guy who got his hand caught in the door of their bus.

An interesting development occurred with Knobby that almost approached being more painful to the regulars in camp than to Knobby. They envisioned the sanctity of their environment being encroached. Elsie Carlson and her husband, Frank, used to own the bakery goods store in town. Knobby remembered it well when he was younger and had a craving for sweet stuff. Frank died and the widow Carlson finally sold the bakery goods store. After a few years of inactivity she began looking for a husband and for some reason set her sights on Knobby. It was rumored that Jailer John told her that he was available. One day the Jailer took her with him to visit Knobby's and she brought along a batch of her famous homemade ginger cookies that Knobby used to enjoy.

It had been several years since they had seen each other and their first meeting was a friendly reacquaintance. Following that almost every week the Jailer drove Elsie to Knobby's and she brought a batch of cookies or some of her other goodies. Everyone knew she had set her eyes on Knobby.

"You taking a liking to widow Carlson?" Ralph asked Knobby one day.

"Not on your life."

"Well, she sure has made it clear that she wants to get hitched again," Ralph said, "and to you."

"Not to me," Knobby replied.

"The Jailer says she's putting her house up for sale because she's going to move in with you."

"Well, she's got another think coming," Knobby said abruptly.

On one of her courting trips widow Carlson told Knobby she would bring him one of her delicious scalloped potato dishes and maybe he could spare a few potatoes from his garden.

"The Jailer told me you grew the best potatoes around," she said to Knobby.

"I work at it," he said.

Ralph was handling the bar in the Lounge and heard the conversation.

"Well, if you could dig up some of your choice potatoes, I'll see that you get a scalloped potato dinner worthy of a king."

"You got a deal," Knobby said and went to the bar and told Ralph to dig up some of the best potatoes for the widow Carlson before she left.

Ralph dug up enough potatoes to fill a burlap sack. He put them in the official car Jailer John was using to provide transportation for Elsie to and from Knobby's.

"Next week, Knobby, dear I'll bring you the kind of meal you've been missing for all these years," the widow Carlson said smiling.

She didn't show up next week or the week after. Knobby was more relaxed but did wonder what happened to the scalloped potato dinner she was going to bring. Jailer John pulled in one day, walked into the Lounge and said to Knobby, "Well, you sure lost your meal ticket with Elsie Carlson."

"What do you mean?" asked Knobby.

"She's got her eye on Tom Schumaker now and it looks like old Tom has taken a shine to her and her cooking."

Knobby was surprised but also a little disheartened to learn that he was no longer Number One. "How did all that happen?" he asked.

"Seems she didn't appreciate the potatoes you gave her," the Jailer said.

"Potatoes!"

"Everyone of them in the sack were hollow."

Knobby looked over at Ralph who suddenly became very busy moving glasses from one shelf to another. Later that night Knobby went up to Ralph and said, "Thanks."

The first significant inroad that old age made at Knobby's occurred one morning when Sam the Chummer didn't go out fishing. He had been with Ralph at his place the night before and some thought Sam might be sleeping in. But by the time noon came around and Sam still wasn't out messing in his boat or looking in garbage cans, Ralph went to Cedar Rest to see what was wrong. Ralph found Sam still in bed and no longer among the living. Sam had died in his sleep.

Knobby contacted the Ackerman family and they told Knobby to make all the arrangements. When Knobby and some of the others went through Sam's stuff they found a piece of paper that was legal enough to be Sam's will. It specified that he wanted to be cremated and his ashes strewn over the lake, preferably around his plastic markers. The paper also provided that Ralph LeBlanc inherit all of Sam Ackerman's worldly assets including the yellow Checker cab.

The funeral was held on the dock and Professor Trinkle conducted the services. It was his finest hour, and Sam would have been proud at the way he was eulogized. Knobby, Ralph, and Big Joe motored out over the lake and chummed Sam's ashes in various places much like Sam would have chummed those spots himself. On the way back they picked up all the plastic bottles they could find.

Then they all gathered in the Lounge afterwards. Knobby told them the drinks would be on the house and that they were going to have one helluva wake for old Sam the Chummer. Ralph interrupted Knobby and said, "We sure are but the drinks are on me."

Sam's funeral was like changing the guard at Knobby's. It was the last any of them would see of the Trinkles. He became diabetic and could hardly walk. The Professor and Pauline were confined to the small college town and finally nobody ever heard anymore about them.

Then Pops Robertson came down ailing and moved far away to where his daughter lived. People lost all contact with him.

Mac McFarland couldn't take the "hard life," as he called it, any longer and he and Marge really slowed down on their fishing. But they always showed up when their son and his family spent two weeks at Knobby's. And Mac never lost this bravado. "For Crisake, Marge. These kids can't fish like you and I did."

New generations of the Italian Connection started coming to Knobby's. There was Locicero, Caproni, Pulozzi, Pigntiello moving into Breezy Point just as unscheduled as in previous years. Instead of arriving in a big black Cadillac they pulled in driving a fancy motorhome but Knobby never yelled, "Park that thing off the road between the cabins." It would stand idle in front of Breezy Point with people amazed and envious of all its motorized conveniences. Occasionally, they arrived driving a fully equipped four door stretch-type Mercedes sedan or a customized BMW. One thing about this generation of the Italian Connection was that they fished when most sensible people fished and never at night.

The Polishers still come in droves. Kalinowski, Greski, Sledziewski, Niemyski and others would jump out of their mobile trailer they now drove much like they used to exit from the bus, but they still had to park it between the cabins. And oddly enough, these Ski's would have no part of skinny scavenger fish. It it wasn't walleyes, perch, bass, they released it.

An interesting group of newcomers started showing up and they were caught up with the fishing fever as much as any group. It didn't take long for them to acquire a name as people started calling them the Hoses. "Que pasa?" they always asked when meeting someone in camp. The foursome of Sanchez, Rodriguez, Chavez, and Hernandez were indeed a fun-loving bunch and would occasionally delight the camp with a variety of Mexican dances whenever they had too much tequila. Once they asked Ralph if he would like to try some of the burritos they cooked up in their cabin. Ralph would try most any food offered him. His first bite was non-committal even after he swallowed. His second and the third bites torched his tongue and tears developed in his eyes as the salsa and the red chili penetrated his taste buds. Ralph fanned his mouth, rushed for the water tap, and gulped down a glass of water. Even his forehead that never got much sun was now quite red.

"No mas?"

"Holy Bejeesus, that's hotten' than a bull in fly time." He

bolted out the door and went to the Lounge where he had a few cold beers.

It wasn't the burrito that slowed Ralph down. The aging process was also catching up with him and he started spending more time in his tarpaper shanty sitting in his big stuffed chair just gazing at the walls. With all he inherited from Sam, he hardly spent a cent and continued to live in his shanty. The only time he would squander any money was when he bought a round or two in the Lounge.

Ralph no longer did the odd jobs around camp. Jailer John brought in a destitute wanderer one day that he had picked up in town and asked Knobby if he could find work for him and a place to stay. This guy was much like Polack John except he didn't say "Guddum, Guddum, Sumbich." Knobby had him take over the work Ralph was doing and had him stay in the bunk house. This guy worked out very well although he was a little slow upstairs. Most of the gang here now at Knobby's started calling him "Dewey" because he did so many things so well. Ralph was not so sure of that and he would walk through camp every other day inspecting the things Dewey was doing to make sure they were up to LeBlanc's standards. But Knobby took a shine to his young man as if he were the son he never had, and much like Jack the Bum had befriended him.

An interesting development occurred with Jailer John, which may or may not be related to the aging process unless you would want to refer to it as the "mellowing process." He resigned his job as constable and moved in with DeeDee Duval. They never got married but that mattered not. She was coughing more and louder. *Haaawwwk, Haaawwwk.* Jimmy Murphy, the railroad brakeman died, and the Jailer just thought she needed someone around the house. DeeDee still made pies but no more tarts since Jailer moved in, and she still had people drop in to play cards and have refreshments

in her living room. Most people looked kindly at the Jailer wanting to help out like he did. All except Moose Weinantz who jealously would tell all within listening distance, "All Jailer's interested in is catching that Killer Bass. And to think, old DeeDee could have had me."

Yes, the guard was changing and it was a natural and compatible evolution. The fishing tackle was becoming more sophisticated, the equipment more powerful, and the old-timers didn't adjust too readily. They continued to use their old stuff and caught just as much as anyone else. Knobby still rented boats but most people were now towing in their own deluxe models. What used to take hours to cover the Lake of Six Rivers was now done in minutes. Whenever the old-timer regulars showed up, they started to notice that Lake of Six

Rivers wasn't as big as they first remembered it to be or the trees as large or the fish as big or plentiful. But the one element that was constant with them was the stories they told. They were always the same, full of energy and unforgettable. And ultimately it would be the same with the new guard.

Garnett Hubert Noblitt one cool afternoon walked past Whispering Pines cabin into the woods behind camp. He brushed past the pine boughs and gingerly stepped over the deadfalls until he found the mound and large stone that marked Jack Tackett's grave. He knelt on the ground, removed an accumulation of twigs and leaves then sat for a long spell in the quiet. Finally, with a fullness in his throat, Knobby said, "Jack, with all that God gave us I think He would be proud of what we did."